A R N E

ARNE

BJÖRNSTJERNE BJÖRNSON

Translated from the Norse
By
RASMUS B. ANDERSON

Fredonia Books
Amsterdam, The Netherlands

Arne

by
Björnstjerne Björnson

ISBN: 1-4101-0332-3

Reprinted from the 1882 edition

Fredonia Books
Amsterdam, The Netherlands
http://www.fredoniabooks.com

In order to make original editions of historical works available to scholars at an economical price, this facsimile of the original edition of 1882 is reproduced from the best available copy and has been digitally enhanced to improve legibility, but the text remains unaltered to retain historical authenticity.

PREFACE.

"ARNE" was written in 1858, one year later than "Synnöve Solbakken," and is thought by many to be Björnson's best story, though it is, in my opinion, surpassed in simplicity of style and delicate analysis of motives, feelings, and character by "A Happy Boy," his third long story, the translation of which is now in progress, and which will follow this volume.

Norway's most eminent composers have written music for many of Björnson's poems, and made them favorite songs, not only with the cultivated classes, but also with the common people. To the songs in "Arne" melodies were composed by Björnson's brilliant cousin, Rikard Nordraak, who died in 1865, only twenty-three years old, but who had already won a place as one of Norway's greatest composers.

With a view of popularizing these melodies in this country, all the poems have been given in precisely the same metre and rhyme as the original, and those caring to know how the tunes are supposed to have sounded on the lips of Arne are referred to "The Norway Music Album," edited by Auber Forestier and myself, and published by Oliver Ditson & Co. of

6 PREFACE.

Boston. In it will be found, together with the original and English words, Rikard Nordraak's music to
the following five songs from "Arne" : —

1. "Oh, my pet lamb, lift your head," from chapter v.

2. "It was such a pleasant, sunny day," from chapter viii.

3. "The tree's early leaf-buds were bursting their
brown," from chapter xii.

4. "Oh how I wonder what I should see

     Over the lofty mountains,"[1] from chapter
     xiv.

5. "He went in the forest the whole day long,"
from chapter xiv.

Mr. Björnson returned to Norway in May, 1881;
he was welcomed with enthusiasm, and on the 17th
of the same month, Norway's natal day, he delivered
the oration at the dedication of the Wergeland Monu-
ment to a gathering of more than ten thousand people. His visit to America was a brilliant success.
His addresses to his countrymen in America were
chiefly on the constitutional struggle of Norway, on
which subject an article by him will be found in the
February (1881) issue of "Scribner's Monthly." As
a souvenir of his pleasant sojourn among us, I will
here attempt an English translation of the poem
"Olaf Trygvason" with which he usually greeted his
hearers at his lectures. It is one of his most popular
songs.

[1] To this there will also be found in the Album a melody by
Halfdan Kjerulf.

Spreading sails o'er the North Sea speed;
High on deck stands at dawn, indeed,
Erling Skjalgson from Sole.
Spying o'er the sea towards Denmark:
"Wherefore comes not Olaf Trygvason?"

Six and fifty the dragons are;
Sails are furled . . . . toward Denmark stare
Sun-scorchèd men . . . . then rises:
"Where stays the King's Long Serpent?
Wherefore comes not Olaf Trygvason?"

But when sun on the second day
Saw the watery, mastless way,
Like a great storm it sounded:
"Where stays the King's Long Serpent?
Wherefore comes not Olaf Trygvason?"

Quiet, quiet, in that same hour
Stood they all; for with endless power,
Groaning, the sea was splashing:
"Taken the King's Long Serpent!
Fallen is Olaf Trygvason!"

Thus for more than an hundred years
Sounds in every seaman's ears,
Chiefly in moon-lit watches:
"Taken the King's Long Serpent!
Fallen is Olaf Trygvason!"

The reader will not fail to be reminded by this song by Björnson of Longfellow's "Saga of King Olaf" (the Musician's Tale), in his "Tales of a Wayside Inn," and especially of those beautiful poems in this collection, "The Building of the Long Serpent," and "The Crew of the Long Serpent."

Hoping the translation of these stories and songs

will enable the reader to appreciate in some degree
the secret of Björnson's great popularity in the fair
land that lies beneath the eternal snow and the un-
setting sun, I now offer "Arne" to the American
public.

RASMUS B. ANDERSON.

ASGARD, MADISON, WIS.,
    August, 1881.

CHAPTER I.

THERE was a deep gorge between two
mountains; through this gorge a large, full
stream flowed heavily over a rough and stony
bottom. Both sides were high and steep,
and so one side was bare; but close to its
foot, and so near the stream that the latter
sprinkled it with moisture every spring and
autumn, stood a group of fresh-looking trees,
gazing upward and onward, yet unable to advance this way or that.

"What if we should clothe the mountain?"
said the juniper one day to the foreign oak, to
which it stood nearer than all the others. The
oak looked down to find out who it was that
spoke, and then it looked up again without
deigning a reply. The river rushed along so
violently that it worked itself into a white
foam; the north wind had forced its way
through the gorge and shrieked in the clefts
of the rocks; the naked mountain, with its
great weight, hung heavily over and felt cold.
"What if we should clothe the mountain?"

said the juniper to the fir on the other side.
"If anybody is to do it, I suppose it must be
we," said the fir, taking hold of its beard and
glancing toward the birch. "What do you
think?" But the birch peered cautiously up
at the mountain, which hung over it so threat-
eningly that it seemed as if it could scarcely
breathe. "Let us clothe it in God's name!"
said the birch. And so, though there were but
these three, they undertook to clothe the mountain. The juniper went first.

When they had gone a little way, they met
the heather. The juniper seemed as though
about to go past it. "Nay, take the heather
along," said the fir. And the heather joined
them. Soon it began to glide on before the
juniper. "Catch hold of me," said the heather.
The juniper did so, and where there was only a
wee crevice, the heather thrust in a finger,
and where it first had placed a finger, the juniper took hold with its whole hand. They
crawled and crept along, the fir laboring on behind, the birch also. "This is well worth doing," said the birch.

But the mountain began to ponder on what
manner of insignificant objects these might be
that were clambering up over it. And after it
had been considering the matter a few hundred

years it sent a little brook down to inquire. It
was yet in the time of the spring freshets, and
the brook stole on until it reached the heather.
" Dear, dear heather, cannot you let me pass; I
am so small." The heather was very busy;
only raised itself a little and pressed onward.
In, under, and onward went the brook. " Dear,
dear juniper, cannot you let me pass ; I am so
small." The juniper looked sharply at it; but
if the heather had let it pass, why, in all reason, it must do so too. Under it and onward
went the brook; and now came to the spot
where the fir stood puffing on the hill-side.
" Dear, dear fir, cannot you let me pass ; I am
really so small," said the brook, — and it kissed
the fir's foot and made itself so very sweet.
The fir became bashful at this, and let it pass.
But the birch raised itself before the brook
asked it. " Hi, hi, hi ! " said the brook and
grew. " Ha, ha, ha ! " said the brook and grew.
" Ho, ho, ho ! " said the brook, and flung the
heather and the juniper and the fir and the
birch flat on their faces and backs, up and
down these great hills. The mountain sat for
many hundred years musing on whether it had
not smiled a little that day.

It was plain enough : the mountain did not
want to be clad. The heather fretted over

this until it grew green again, and then it started forward. " Fresh courage ! " said the heather.

The juniper had half raised itself to look at the heather, and continued to keep this position, until at length it stood upright. It scratched its head and set forth again, taking such a vigorous foothold that it seemed as though the mountain must feel it. " If you will not have me, then I will have you." The fir crooked its toes a little to find out whether they were whole, then lifted one foot, found it whole, then the other, which proved also to be whole, then both of them. It first investigated the ground it had been over, next where it had been lying, and finally where it should go. After this it began to wend its way slowly along, and acted just as though it had never fallen. The birch had become most wretchedly soiled, but now rose up and made itself tidy. Then they sped onward, faster and faster, upward and on either side, in sunshine and in rain. " What in the world can this be ? " said the mountain, all glittering with dew, as the summer sun shone down on it, — the birds sang, the wood-mouse piped, the hare hopped along, and the ermine hid itself and screamed.

Then the day came when the heather could

peep with one eye over the edge of the mountain. "Oh dear, oh dear, oh dear!" said the heather, and away it went. "Dear me! what is it the heather sees?" said the juniper, and moved on until it could peer up. "Oh dear, oh dear!" it shrieked, and was gone. "What is the matter with the juniper to-day?" said the fir, and took long strides onward in the heat of the sun. Soon it could raise itself on its toes and peep up. "Oh dear!" Branches and needles stood on end in wonderment. It worked its way forward, came up, and was gone. "What is it all the others see, and not I?" said the birch; and, lifting well its skirts, it tripped after. It stretched its whole head up at once. "Oh, — oh! — is not here a great forest of fir and heather, of juniper and birch, standing upon the table-land waiting for us?" said the birch; and its leaves quivered in the sunshine so that the dew trembled. "Aye, this is what it is to reach the goal!" said the juniper.

CHAPTER II.

UP on the hill-top it was that Arne was born. His mother's name was Margit, and she was the only child at the houseman's place, — Kampen.[1] Once, in her eighteenth year, she stayed too long at a dance; her companions had left her, and so Margit thought that the way home would be just as long whether she waited until the dancing was over or not. And thus it happened that she kept her seat until the fiddler, known as Nils the tailor, suddenly laid aside his fiddle, as was his wont when drink took possession of him, let others troll the tune, seized the prettiest girl, moved his foot as evenly as the rhythm of a song, and with his boot-heel took the hat from the head of the tallest person present. "Ho!" said he.

When Margit went home that evening, the moon-beams played on the snow with most wondrous beauty. After she had reached her bedchamber she was moved to look out once more.

[1] The top of a hill is called in Norwegian "Kamp," and the houseman's place took its name from its situation.

She took off her boddice, but remained standing with it in her hand. Then she felt that she was cold, closed the door hastily, undressed, and nestled in under the robe. That night Margit dreamed about a great red cow that had wandered into the field. She went to drive it out, but though she tried hard, she could not stir from the spot; the cow stood calmly grazing there until it grew plump and well fed, and every now and then it looked at her, with large, heavy eyes.

The next time there was a dance in the parish Margit was present. She cared little for dancing that evening; she kept her seat to listen to the music, and it seemed strange to her that there were not others also who preferred this. But when the evening had worn on, the fiddler arose and wanted to dance. All at once he went directly to Margit Kampen. She scarcely knew what she was about, but she danced with Nils the tailor.

Soon the weather grew warm, and there was no more dancing. That spring Margit took such interest in a little lamb that had fallen ill, that her mother almost thought she was overdoing it.

" It is only a little lamb," said the mother.

" Yes, but it is ill," replied Margit.

It was some time since she had been to church; she wished to have her mother go, she said, and some one must be at home. One Sunday, later in the summer, the weather was so fine that the hay could well be left out for twenty-four hours, and the mother said that now they surely might both go. Margit could not reasonably object to this, and got ready for church; but when they were so far on their way that they could hear the church-bells, she burst into tears. The mother grew deathly pale: but they went on, the mother in advance, Margit following, listened to the sermon, joined in all the hymns to the very last, followed the prayer, and heard the bell ring before they left. But when they were seated in the family-room at home again, the mother took Margit's face between her hands and said: —

"Hide nothing from me, my child."

There came another winter when Margit did not dance. But Nils the tailor fiddled, took more strong drink than ever, and always, toward the close of the evening, swung the prettiest girl at the party. In those days, it was told as a certain fact that he could marry whom he pleased among the daughters of the first gard-owners in the parish; some added that Eli Böen herself had courted him for her daughter Birgit, who was madly in love with him.

But just at that time an infant of the houseman's daughter at Kampen was brought to baptism ; it was christened Arne, and tailor Nils was spoken of as its father.

The evening of the same day Nils was at a large wedding; there he got drunk. He would not play, but danced all the time, and scarcely brooked having others on the floor. But when he crossed to Birgit Böen and asked her to dance, she declined. He gave a short laugh, turned on his heel, and caught hold of the first girl he encountered. She resisted. He looked down ; it was a little dark maiden who had been sitting gazing fixedly at him, and who was now pale. Bowing lightly over her, he whispered, —

" Will you not dance with *me*, Karen ? "

She made no reply. He asked once more. Then she answered in a whisper, as he had asked, —

" *That* dance might go farther than I wished."

He drew slowly back, but once in the middle of the floor, he made a spring and danced the

2

halling [1] alone. No one else was dancing; the others stood looking on in silence.

Afterwards he went out in the barn, and there he lay down and wept.

Margit kept at home with the little boy. She heard about Nils, how he went from dance to dance, and she looked at the child and wept, — looked at him again and was happy. The first thing she taught him was to say papa; but this she dared not do when the mother, or the grandmother, as she was henceforth called, chanced to be near. The result of this was that it was the grandmother whom the boy called papa. It cost Margit much to break him of this, and thus she fostered in him an early shrewdness. He was not very large before he knew that Nils the tailor was his father, and when he reached the age in which the romantic acquires a flavor, he became also aware what sort of a man tailor Nils was. The grandmother had strictly forbidden even the mention of his name; what she mainly strove for was to have the houseman's place, Kampen, become an independent gard, so that her daughter and her boy might be free from care. She availed herself of the gard-owner's poverty, effected the purchase of

[1] A popular dance in two-fourths time, described in this chapter.

the place, paid off a portion of the money each
year, and managed the business like a man, for
she had been a widow for fourteen years.
Kampen was a large place, and had been ex-
tended until now it fed four cows, sixteen
sheep, and a horse in which she was half owner.

Nils the tailor meanwhile took to roving
about the parish; his business had fallen off,
partly because he felt less interest in it, partly
also because he was not liked as before. He
gave, therefore, more time to fiddling; this led
oftener to drinking and thence to fighting and
evil days. There were those who had heard
him say he was unhappy.

Arne might have been about six years old,
when one winter day he was frolicking in the
bed, whose coverlet he had up for a sail, while
he was steering with a ladle. The grandmother
sat spinning in the room, absorbed in her own
thoughts, and nodded occasionally as though
she would make a fixed fact of something she
was thinking about. The boy knew that he
was unheeded, and he fell to singing, just as he
had learned it, the rough, wild song about
tailor Nils: —

" Unless 't was only yesterday hither first you came,
   You 've surely heard already of Nils the tailor's fame.

' Unless 't was but this morning you came among us first,
   You 've heard how he knocked over tall Johan Knutson Kirst·

" How, in his famous barn-fight with Ola Stor-Johann,
  He said, ' Bring down your porridge when we two fight again.'

" That fighting fellow, Bugge, a famous man was he:
  His name was known all over fjord and fell and sea.

" ' Now, choose the place, you tailor, where I shall knock you
    down,
  And then I 'll spit upon it, and there I 'll lay your crown.'

" ' Ah, only come so near, I may catch your scent, my man,
  Your bragging hurts nobody; don't dream it ever can.'

" The first round was a poor one, and neither man could beat;
  But both kept in their places, and steady on their feet.

" The second round, poor Bugge was beaten black and blue.
  ' Little Bugge, are you tired? It 's going hard with you.'

" The third round, Bugge tumbled, and bleeding there he lay.
  Now, Bugge, where 's your bragging?' ' Bad luck to me
    to-day!'"[1]

More the boy did not sing; but there were
two other stanzas which his mother was not
likely to have taught him : —

" Have you seen a tree cast its shadow on yesterday's snow?
  Have you seen how Nils does his smiles on the girls bestow?

" Have you looked at Nils when to dance he just commences?
  Come, my girl, you must go; it is too late, when you 've lost
    your senses."

These two stanzas the grandmother knew,
and they came all the more distinctly into her
mind because they were not sung. She said

[1] Translated by Augusta Plesner and S. Rugeley-Powers.

nothing to the boy; but to the mother she said, " Teach the boy well about your own shame; do not forget the last verses."

Nils the tailor was so broken down by drink that he was no longer the man he had been, and some people thought his end could not be far distant.

It so happened that two American gentlemen were visiting in the parish, and having heard that a wedding was going on in the vicinity, wanted to attend it, that they might learn the customs of the country. Nils was playing there. They gave each a dollar to the fiddler, and asked for a halling; but no one would come forward to dance it, however much it was urged. Several begged Nils himself to dance. " He was best, after all,' they said. He refused, but the request became still more urgent, and finally unanimous. This was what he wanted. He gave his fiddle to another player, took off his jacket and cap, and stepped smiling into the middle of the room. He was followed by the same eager attention as of old, and this gave him his old strength. The people crowded closely together, those who were farthest back climbing upon tables and benches. Some of the girls were perched up higher than all the rest, and foremost among

these — a tall girl with sunny brown hair of
a varying tint, with blue eyes deeply set beneath a strong forehead, a large mouth that
often smiled, drawing a little to one side as
it did so — was Birgit Böen. Nils saw her,
as he glanced up at the beam. The music
struck up, a deep silence followed, and he
began. He dashed forward along the floor, his
body inclining to one side, half aslant, keeping
time to the fiddle. Crouching down, he bal-
anced himself, now on one foot, now on the
other, flung his legs crosswise under him,
sprang up again, stood as though about to make
a fling, and then moved on aslant as before.
The fiddle was handled by skillful fingers, and
more and more fire was thrown into the tune.
Nils threw his head farther and farther back,
and suddenly his boot-heel touched the beam,
sending the dust from the ceiling in showers
over them all. The people laughed and
shouted about him; the girls stood well-nigh
breathless. The tune hurrahed with the rest,
stimulating him anew with more and more
strongly-marked accents, nor did he resist the
exciting influences. He bent forward, hopped
along in time to the music, made ready appar
ently for a fling, but only as a hoax, and then
moved on, his body aslant as before; and when

he seemed the least prepared for it, his boot-
heel thundered against the beam again and
again, whereupon he turned summersaults for-
wards and backwards in the air, landing each
time erect on his feet. He broke off abruptly,
and the tune, running through some wild varia-
tions, worked its way down to a deep tone in
the bass, where it quivered and vibrated, and
died away with a long-drawn stroke of the bow.
The crowd dispersed, and loud, eager conversation, mingled with shouts and exclamations,
broke the silence. Nils stood leaning against
the wall, and the American gentlemen went
over to him, with their interpreter, and each
gave him five dollars.

The Americans talked a little with the interpreter, whereupon the latter asked Nils if he
would go with them as their servant; he should
have whatever wages he wanted. "Whither?"
asked Nils. The people crowded about them
as closely as possible. "Out into the world,"
was the reply. "When?" asked Nils, and
looking around with a shining face, he caught
Birgit Böen's eyes, and did not let them go
again. "In a week, when we come back here,"
was the answer. "It is possible I will be
ready," replied Nils, weighing his two five-dollar
pieces. He had rested one arm on the shoulder

of a man standing near him, and it trembled so that the man wanted to help him to the bench.

"It is nothing," replied Nils, made some wavering steps across the floor, then some firm ones, and, turning, asked for a spring-dance.[1]

All the girls had come to the front. Casting a long, lingering look about him, he went straightway to one of them in a dark skirt; it was Birgit Böen. He held out his hand, and she gave him both of hers; then he laughed, drew back, caught hold of the girl beside her, and danced away with perfect abandon. The blood coursed up in Birgit's neck and face. A tall man, with a mild countenance, was standing directly behind her; he took her by the hand and danced off after Nils. The latter saw this, and — it might have been only through heedlessness — he danced so hard against them that the man and Birgit were sent reeling over and fell heavily on the floor. Shouting and laughter arose about them. Birgit got up at last, went aside, and wept bitterly.

The man with the mild face rose more slowly and went straight over to Nils, who was still dancing. "You had better stop a little," said the man. Nils did not hear, and then the man

---

[1] A popular dance, in three-fourths time.

took him by the arm. Nils tore himself away
and looked at him. "I do not know you," said
he, with a smile. "No; but you shall learn to
know me," said the man with the mild face, and
with this he struck Nils a blow over one eye.
Nils, who was wholly unprepared for this, was
plunged heavily across the sharp-edged hearth-
stone, and when he promptly tried to rise, he
found that he could not; his back was broken.

At Kampen a change had taken place. The
grandmother had been growing very feeble of
late, and when she realized this she strove
harder than ever to save money enough to pay
off the last installment on the gard. "Then
you and the boy will have all you need," she
said to her daughter. "And if you let any one
come in and waste it for you, I will turn in my
grave." During the autumn, too, she had the
pleasure of being able to stroll up to the former
head-gard with the last remaining portion of
the debt, and happy was she when she had
taken her seat again, and could say, "Now that
is done!" But at that very time she was at-
tacked by her last illness; she betook herself
forthwith to her bed, and never rose again.
Her daughter buried her in a vacant spot in the
churchyard, and placed over her a handsome
cross, whereon was inscribed her name and age,

with a verse from one of Kingo's [1] hymns. A fortnight after the grandmother was laid in her grave, her Sunday gown was made over into clothes for the boy, and when he put them on, he became as solemn as though he were his grandmother come back again. Of his own accord, he went to the book with big print and large clasps she had read and sung from every Sunday, opened it, and there inside found her spectacles. These the boy had never been permitted to touch during his grandmother's lifetime; now he timidly took them up, put them on his nose, and looked through them into the book. All was misty. "How strange," thought the boy, "it was through them grandmother could read the word of God." He held them high up toward the light to see what the matter was, and — the spectacles lay on the floor.

He was much alarmed, and when the door at that moment opened, it seemed to him as though his grandmother must be coming in, but it was his mother, and behind her, six men, who, with much tramping and noise, were bearing in a litter, which they placed in the middle of the floor. For a long time the door was left open, so that it grew cold in the room.

On the litter lay a man with dark hair and

[1] A Dane, the most noted psalmist of Scandinavia.

pale face; the mother moved about weeping. "Lay him carefully on the bed," she begged, herself lending a helping hand. But while the men were moving with him, something made a noise under their feet. "Oh, it is only grandmother's spectacles," thought the boy, but he did not say so.

CHAPTER III.

IT was in the autumn, as before stated. A week after Nils the tailor was borne into Margit Kampen's home, there came word to him from the Americans that he must hold himself in readiness to start. He lay just then writhing under a terrible attack of pain, and, gnashing his teeth, he shrieked, "Let them go to hell!" Margit stood motionless, as though he had made no answer. He noticed this, and presently he repeated slowly and feebly, "Let them — go."

As the winter advanced, he improved so much that he was able to sit up, although his health was shattered for life. The first time he actually sat up, he took out his fiddle and tuned it, but became so agitated that he had to go to bed again. He grew very taciturn, but was not hard to get along with; and as time wore on, he taught the boy to read, and began to take work in at home. He never went out, and would not talk with those who dropped in to see him. At first Margit used to bring him the

parish news ; he was always gloomy afterwards,
so she ceased to do so.

When spring had fairly set in, he and Margit would sit longer than usual talking together
after the evening meal. The boy was then sent
off to bed. Some time later in the spring their
bans were published in church, after which they
were quietly married.

He did his share of work in the fields now,
and managed everything in a sensible, orderly
way. Margit said to the boy, " There is both
profit and pleasure in him. Now you must be
obedient and good, that you may do your best
for him."

Margit had remained tolerably stout through
all her sorrow ; she had a ruddy face and very
large eyes, which looked all the larger because
there was a ring round them. She had full
lips, a round face, and looked healthy and
strong, although she was not very strong. At
this period of her life, she was looking better
than ever ; and she always sang when she was
at work, as had ever been her wont.

One Sunday afternoon, father and son went
out to see how the crops were thriving that
year. Arne ran about his father, shooting with
a bow and arrow. Nils had himself made
them for the boy. Thus they passed on directly

up toward the road leading past the church
and parsonage, down to what was called the
broad valley. Nils seated himself on a stone
by the roadside and fell to dreaming ; the boy
shot into the road and sprang after his arrow,—
it was in the direction of the church. "Not
too far away!" said the father. While the
boy was playing there, he paused, as though
listening. "Father, I hear music!" The
father listened too ; they heard the sounds of
fiddling, almost drowned at times by loud
shouts and wild uproar ; but above all rose the
steady rumbling of cart-wheels and the clat-
ter of horses' feet ; it was a bridal procession,
wending its way home from church. "Come
here, boy," shouted the father, and Arne knew
by the tones of the voice that he must make
haste. The father had hurriedly risen and
hidden behind a large tree. The boy hastened after him. "Not here, over there!" cried
the father, and the boy stepped behind an
alder-copse. Already the carts were winding
round the birch-grove ; they came at a wild
speed, the horses were white with foam, drunken
people were crying and shouting ; father and
son counted cart after cart,— there were in all
fourteen. In the first sat two fiddlers, and the
wedding march sounded merrily through the

clear air, — a boy stood behind and drove.
Afterwards came a crowned bride, who sat on
a high seat and glittered in the sunshine ; she
smiled, and her mouth drew to one side ; beside
her sat a man clad in blue and with a mild face.
The bridal train followed, the men sat on the
women's laps ; small boys were sitting behind,
drunken men were driving, — there were six
people to one horse ; the man who presided at
the feast came in the last cart, holding a keg of
brandy on his lap. They passed by screaming
and singing, and drove recklessly down the
hill ; the fiddling, the voices, the rattling of
wheels, lingered behind them in the dust ; the
breeze bore up single shrieks, soon only a dull
rumbling, and then nothing. Nils stood motionless ; there was a rustling behind him, he
turned ; it was the boy who was creeping forward.

" Who was it, father ? " But the boy started, for his father's face was dreadful. Arne
stood motionless waiting for an answer ; then
he remained where he was because he got none.
After some time he became impatient and ven-
tured again. " Shall we go ? " Nils was still
gazing after the bridal train, but he now con-
trolled himself and started on. Arne followed
after. He put an arrow into the bow, shot it.

and ran. "Do not trample down the grass,'
said Nils gruffly. The boy let the arrow lie
and came back. After a while he had forgotten this, and once when his father paused, he
lay down and turned summersaults. "Do not
trample down the grass, I say." Here Arne
was seized by one arm, and lifted by it with
such violence that it was almost put out of
joint. Afterward, he walked quietly behind.

At the door Margit awaited them; she had
just come in from the stable, where she had evidently had pretty hard work, for her hair was
tumbled, her linen soiled, her dress likewise,
but she stood in the door smiling. "A couple
of the cows got loose and have been into mis-
chief; now they are tied again."

"You might make yourself a little tidy on
Sunday," said Nils, as he went past into the
house.

"Yes, there is some sense in tidying up now
that the work is done," said Margit, and followed him. She began to fix herself at once,
and sang while she was doing so. Now Margit
sang well, but sometimes there was a little
huskiness in her voice.

"Stop that screaming," said Nils; he had
thrown himself on his back across the bed.
Margit stopped.

Then the boy came storming in. "There has come into the yard a great black dog, a dreadful looking" —

"Hold your tongue, boy," said Nils from the bed, and thrust out one foot to stamp on the floor with it. "A devilish noise that boy is always making," he muttered afterward, and drew his foot up again.

The mother held up a warning finger to the boy. "You surely must see that father is not in a good humor," she meant. "Will you not have some strong coffee with syrup in it?" said she; she wanted to put him in a good humor again. This was a drink the grandmother had liked, and the rest of them too. Nils did not like it at all, but had drunk it because the others did so. "Will you not have some strong coffee with syrup in it?" repeated Margit; for he had made no reply the first time. Nils raised himself up on both elbows and shrieked, 'Do you think I will pour down such slops?"

Margit was struck with surprise, and, taking the boy with her, went out.

They had a number of things to attend to outside, and did not come in before suppertime. Then Nils was gone. Arne was sent out into the field to call him, but found him nowhere. They waited until the supper was

nearly cold, then ate, and still Nils had not
come. Margit became uneasy, sent the boy to
bed, and sat down to wait. A little after midnight Nils appeared.

" Where have you been, dear ? " asked she.

" That is none of your business," he answered, and slowly sat down on the bench.

He was drunk.

After this, Nils often went out in the parish,
and always came home drunk. " I cannot stand
it at home here with you," said he once when
he came in. She tried gently to defend herself,
and then he stamped on the floor and bade her
be silent: if he was drunk, it was her fault; if
he was wicked, it was her fault too; if he was
a cripple and an unfortunate being for his whole
life, why, she was to blame too, and that infernal boy of hers.

" Why were you always dangling after me ? "
said he, and wept. " What harm had I done
you that you could not leave me in peace ? "

" Lord have mercy on me ! " said Margit.
" Was it I who went after you ? "

" Yes, it was ! " he shrieked as he arose, and
amid tears he continued: " You have succeeded
in getting what you wanted. I drag myself
about from tree to tree. I go every day and
look at my own grave. But I could have lived

in splendor with the finest gard girl in the
parish. I might have traveled as far as the sun
goes, had not you and your damned boy put
yourselves in my way."

She tried again to defend herself. " It was,
at all events, not the boy's fault."

"If you do not hold your tongue, I will
strike you!" — and he struck her.

After he had slept himself sober the next
day, he was ashamed, and was especially kind
to the boy. But soon he was drunk again, and
then he struck the mother. At last he got to
striking her almost every time he was drunk.
The boy cried and lamented; then he struck
him too. Sometimes his repentance was so
deep that he felt compelled to leave the house.
About this time his fondness for dancing revived. He began to go about fiddling as in former days, and took the boy with him to carry
the fiddle-case. Thus Arne saw a great deal.
The mother wept because he had to go along,
but dared not say so to the father. " Hold
faithfully to God, and learn nothing evil," she
begged, and tenderly caressed her boy. But
at the dances there was a great deal of diver-
sion; at home with the mother there was none
at all. Arne turned more and more from her
and to the father: she saw this and was silent.

At the dances Arne learned many songs, and
he sang them at home to his father; this
amused the latter, and now and then the boy
could even get him to laugh. This was so flat-
tering to Arne that he exerted himself to learn
as many songs as possible; soon he noticed
what kind the father liked best, and what it
was that made him laugh. When there was
not enough of this element in the songs he was
singing, the boy added to it himself, and this
early gave him practice in adapting words to
music. It was chiefly lampoons and odious
things about people who had risen to power and
prosperity, that the father liked and the boy
sang.

The mother finally concluded to take him
with her to the stable of evenings; numerous
were the pretexts he found to escape going, but
when, nevertheless, she managed to take him
with her, she talked kindly to him about God
and good things, usually ending by taking him
in her arms, and, amid blinding tears, begging
him, entreating him not to become a bad man.

The mother taught the boy to read, and he
was surprisingly quick at learning. The father
was proud of this, and, especially when he was
drunk, told Arne he had his head.

Soon the father fell into the habit, when

drink got the better of him, of calling on Arne
at dancing-parties to sing for the people. The
boy always obeyed, singing song after song
amid laughter and uproar; the applause pleased
the son almost more than it did the father, and
finally there was no end to the songs Arne
could sing. Anxious mothers who heard this,
went themselves to his mother and told her of
it; their reason for so doing being that the
character of these songs was not what it should
be. The mother put her arms about her boy
and forbade him, in the name of God and all
that was sacred, to sing such songs, and now it
seemed to Arne that everything he took delight
in his mother opposed. For the first time he
told his father what his mother had said. She
had to suffer for this the next time the father
was drunk; he held his peace until then. But
no sooner had it become clear to the boy what
he had done than in his soul he implored par-
don of God and her; he could not bring himself to do so in spoken words. His mother was
just as kind as ever to him, and this cut him to
the quick.

Once, however, he forgot this. He had a
faculty for mimicking people. Above all, he
could talk and sing as others did. The mother
came in one evening when Arne was entertain-

ing his father with this, and it occurred to the
father, after she had gone out, that the boy
should imitate his mother's singing. Arne refused at first, but his father, who lay over on the
bed and laughed until it shook, insisted finally
that he should sing like his mother. She is
gone, thought the boy, and cannot hear it, and
he mimicked her singing as it sounded sometimes when she was hoarse and choked with
tears. The father laughed until it seemed almost hideous to the boy, and he stopped of himself. Just then the mother came in from the
kitchen ; she looked long and hard at the boy,
as she crossed the floor to a shelf after a milk-
pan and turned to carry it out.

A burning heat ran through his whole body ;
she had heard it all. He sprang down from
the table where he had been sitting, went out,
cast himself on the ground, and it seemed as
though he must bury himself out of sight. He
could not rest, and got up feeling that he must
go farther on. He went past the barn, and behind it sat the mother, sewing on a fine, new
shirt, just for him. She had always been in
the habit of singing a hymn over her work
when she sat sewing, but now she was not singing. She was not weeping, either ; she only
sat and sewed. Arne could bear it no longer

he flung himself down in the grass directly in front of her, looked up at her, and wept and sobbed bitterly. The mother dropped her work and took his head between her hands.

"Poor Arne!" said she, and laid her own beside his. He did not try to say a word, but wept as he had never done before. "I knew you were good at heart," said the mother, and stroked down his hair.

"Mother, you must not say no to what I am going to ask for," was the first thing he could say.

"That you know I cannot do," answered she.

He tried to stop crying, and then stammered out, with his head still in her lap: "Mother, sing something for me."

"My dear, I cannot," said she, softly.

"Mother, sing something for me," begged the boy, "or I believe I will never be able to look at you again."

She stroked his hair, but was silent.

"Mother, sing, sing, I say! Sing," he begged. "or I will go so far away that I will never come home any more."

And while he, now fourteen in his fifteenth year as he was, lay there with his head in his mother's lap, she began to sing over him : —

" Father, stretch forth Thy mighty hand,
    Thy Holy Spirit send yonder:
Bless Thou the child on the lonely strand,
    Nor in its sports let it wander.
Slipp'ry the way, the water deep,—
Lord, in Thy arm but the darling keep,
Then through Thy mercy 't will never
Drown, but with Thee live forever.

" Missing her child, in disquiet sore,
    Much for its safety fearing,
Often the mother calls from her door,
    Never an answer hearing, —
Then comes the thought: where'er it be,
Blessed Lord, it is near to Thee;
Jesus will guide his brother
Home to the anxious mother." [1]

She sang several verses. Arne lay still : there
descended upon him a blessed peace, and under
its influence he felt a refreshing weariness.
The last thing he distinctly heard was about
Jesus : it bore him into the midst of a great
light, and there it seemed as though twelve or
thirteen were singing ; but the mother's voice
rose above them all. A lovelier voice he had
never heard ; he prayed that he might sing
thus. It seemed to him that if he were to sing
right softly he might do so; and now he sang
softly, tried again softly, and still more softly,
and then, rejoiced at the bliss that seemed al
most dawning for him, he joined in with full

[1] Auber Forestier's translation.

voice, and the spell was broken. He awakened, looked about him, listened, but heard nothing, save the everlasting, mighty roar of the force, and the little creek that flowed past the barn, with its low and incessant murmuring. The mother was gone, — she had laid under his head the half-finished shirt and her jacket.

CHAPTER IV.

WHEN the time came to take the herds up into the woods, Arne wanted to tend them. His father objected; the boy had never tended cattle, and he was now in his fifteenth year. But he was so urgent that it was finally arranged as he wished; and the entire spring, summer, and autumn he was in the woods by himself the livelong day, only going home to sleep.

He took his books up there with him. He read and carved letters in the bark of the trees; he went about thinking, longing, and singing. When he came home in the evening his father was often drunk, and beat the mother, cursed her and the parish, and talked about how he might once have journeyed far away. Then the longing for travel entered the boy's mind too. There was no comfort at home, and the books opened other worlds to him; sometimes it seemed as though the air, too, wafted him far away over the lofty mountains

So it happened about midsummer that he

met Kristian, the captain's eldest son, who came
with the servant boy to the woods after the
horses, in order to get a ride home. He was a
few years older than Arne, light-hearted and
gay, unstable in all his thoughts, but nevertheless firm in his resolves. He spoke rapidly and
in broken sentences, and usually about two
things at once; rode horseback without a sad-
dle, shot birds on the wing, went fly-fishing,
and seemed to Arne the goal of his aspirations.
He also had his head full of travel, and told
Arne about foreign lands until everything about
them was radiant. He discovered Arne's fondness for reading, and now carried up to him
those books he had read himself. After Arne
had finished reading these, Kristian brought
him new ones; he sat there himself on Sundays,
and taught Arne how to find his way in the
geography and the map; and all summer and
autumn Arne read until he grew pale and
thin.

In the winter he was allowed to read at
home; partly because he was to be confirmed
the next year, partly because he always knew
how to manage his father. He began to go to
school; but there he took most comfort when
he closed his eyes and fancied himself over his
books at home; besides, there were no longer

any companions for him among the peasant boys.

His father's ill-treatment of the mother increased with years, as did also his fondness for drink and his bodily suffering. And when Arne, notwithstanding this, had to sit and amuse him, in order to furnish the mother with an hour's peace, and then often talk of things he now, in his heart, despised, he felt growing within him a hatred for his father. This he hid far down in his heart, as he did his love for his mother. When he was with Kristian, their talk ran on great journeys and books; even to him he said nothing about how things were at home. But many times after these wide-ranging talks, when he was walking home alone, wondering what might now meet him there, he wept and prayed to God, in the starry heavens, to grant that he might soon be allowed to go away.

In the summer he and Kristian were confirmed. Directly afterward, the latter carried out his plan. His father had to let him go from home and become a sailor. He presented Arne with his books, promised to write often to him, — and went away.

Now Arne was alone.

About this time he was again filled with a

desire to write songs. He no longer patched up old ones; he made new ones, and wove into them all that grieved him most.

But his heart grew too heavy, and his sorrow broke forth in his songs. He now lay through long, sleepless nights, brooding, until he felt sure that he could bear this no longer, but must journey far away, seek Kristian, and not say a word about it to any one. He thought of his mother, and what would become of her, — and he could scarcely look her in the face.

He sat up late one evening reading. When his heart became too gloomy, he took refuge in his books, and did not perceive that they increased the venom. His father was at a wedding, but was expected home that evening; his mother was tired, and dreaded her husband's return; had therefore gone to bed. Arne started up at the sound of a heavy fall in the passage and the rattling of something hard, which struck against the door. It was his father who had come home.

Arne opened the door and looked at him.

" Is that you, my clever boy? Come and help your father up ! "

He was raised up and helped in toward the bench. Arne took up the fiddle-case, carried it in, and closed the door.

"Yes, look at me, you clever boy. I am not handsome now; this is no longer tailor Nils. This I say — to you, that you — never shall drink brandy; it is — the world and the flesh and the devil — He resisteth the proud but giveth grace unto the humble. — Ah, woe, woe is me! — How far it has gone with me!"

He sat still a while, then he sang, weeping, —

> "Merciful Lord, I come to Thee;
> Help, if there can be help for me;
> Though by the mire of sin defiled,
> I 'm still thine own dear ransomed child." [1]

"Lord, I am not worthy that Thou shouldest come under my roof; but speak the word only" — He flung himself down, hid his face in his hands, and sobbed convulsively. Long he lay thus, and then he repeated word for word from the Bible, as he had learned it probably more than twenty years before: "Then she came and worshiped Him, saying, Lord, help me! But he answered and said, It is not meet to take the children's bread, and to cast it to dogs. And she said, Truth, Lord, yet the dogs eat of the crumbs which fall from their master's table!"

He was silent now, and dissolved in a flood of tears.

[1] Translated by Augusta Plesner and S. Rugeley-Powers.

The mother had awakened long since, but had not dared raise her eyes, now that her husband was weeping like one who is saved; she leaned on her elbows and looked up.

But scarcely had Nils descried her, than he shrieked out: " Are you staring at me; you, too? — you want to see, I suppose, what you have brought me to. Aye, this is the way I look, exactly so!" He rose up, and she hid herself under the robe. " No, do not hide, I will find you easily enough," said he, extending his right hand, and groping his way along with outstretched forefinger. " Tickle, tickle!" said he, as he drew off the covers and placed his finger on her throat.

" Father!" said Arne.

" Oh dear! how shriveled up and thin you have grown. There is not much flesh here. Tickle, tickle."

The mother convulsively seized his hand with both of hers, but could not free herself, and so rolled herself into a ball.

" Father!" said Arne.

" So life has come into you now. How she writhes, the fright! Tickle, tickle!"

" Father!" said Arne. The room seemed to swim about him.

" Tickle, I say!"

She let go his hands and gave up.

"Father!" shouted Arne. He sprang to the corner, where stood an axe.

"It is only from obstinacy that you do not scream. You had better not do so either; I have taken such a frightful fancy. Tickle, tickle!"

"Father!" shrieked Arne, seizing the axe, but remained standing as though nailed to the spot, for at that moment the father drew himself up, gave a piercing cry, clutched at his breast, and fell over. "Jesus Christ!" said he, and lay quite still.

Arne knew not where he stood or what he stood over; he waited, as it were, for the room to burst asunder, and for a strong light to break in somewhere. The mother began to draw her breath heavily, as though she were rolling off some great weight. She finally half rose, and saw the father lying stretched out on the floor, the son standing beside him with an axe.

"Merciful Lord, what have you done?" she shrieked, and started up out of bed, threw her skirt about her, and came nearer; then Arne felt as if his tongue were unloosed.

"He fell down himself," said he.

"Arne, Arne, I do not believe you," cried the mother, in a loud, rebuking tone. "Now

Jesus be with you ! " and she flung herself over the corpse, with piteous lamentation.

Now the boy came out of his stupor, and dropping down on his knees, exclaimed, "As surely as I look for mercy from God, he fell as he stood there."

"Then our Lord himself has been here," said she, quietly ; and, sitting on the floor, she fixed her eyes on the corpse.

Nils lay precisely as he fell, stiff, with open eyes and mouth. His hands had drawn near together, as though he had tried to clasp them, but had been unable to do so.

"Take hold of your father, you are so strong, and help me lay him on the bed."

And they took hold of him and laid him on the bed. Margit closed his eyes and mouth, stretched him out and folded his hands.

Mother and son stood and looked at him. All they had experienced until then neither seemed so long nor contained so much as this moment. If the devil himself had been there, the Lord had been there also; the encounter had been short. All the past was now settled.

It was a little after midnight, and they had to be there with the dead man until day dawned. Arne crossed the floor, and made a great fire on the hearth, the mother sat down

by it. And now, as she sat there, it rushed
through her mind how many evil days she had
had with Nils; and then she thanked God, in
a loud, fervent prayer, for what He had done.
"But I have truly had some good days also,"
said she, and wept as though she regretted her
recent thankfulness; and it ended in her taking
the greatest blame on herself who had acted
contrary to God's commandment, out of love
for the departed one, had been disobedient to
her mother, and therefore had been punished
through this sinful love.

Arne sat down directly opposite her. The
mother's eyes were fixed on the bed.

" Arne, you must remember that it was for
your sake I bore it all," and she wept, yearning for a loving word in order to gain a sup-
port against her own self-accusations, and comfort for all coming time. The boy trembled
and could not answer. " You must never leave
me," sobbed she.

Then it came suddenly to his mind what she
had been, in all this time of sorrow, and how
boundless would be her desolation should he,
as a reward for her great fidelity, forsake her
now.

"Never, never!" he whispered, longing to go
to her, yet unable to do so.

They kept their seats, but their tears flowed freely together. She prayed aloud, now for the dead man, now for herself and her boy; and thus, amid prayers and tears, the time passed. Finally she said : —

"Arne, you have such a fine voice, you must sit over by the bed and sing for your father."

And it seemed as though strength was forthwith given him to do so. He got up, and went to fetch a hymn-book, then lit a torch, and with the torch in one hand, the hymn-book in the other, he sat down at the head of the bed and, in a clear voice, sang Kingo's one hundred and twenty-seventh hymn : —

> "Turn from us, gracious Lord, thy dire displeasure!
> Let not thy bloody rod, beyond all measure,
> Chasten thy children, laden with sore oppressions,
> For our transgressions." [1]

[1] Auber Forestier's translation.

CHAPTER V.

ARNE became habitually silent and shy. He tended cattle and made songs. He passed his nineteenth birthday, and still he kept on tending cattle. He borrowed books from the priest and read; but he took interest in nothing else.

The priest sent word to him one day that he had better become a school-master, "because the parish ought to derive benefit from your talents and knowledge." Arne made no reply to this; but the next day, while driving the sheep before him, he made the following song : —

> " Oh, my pet lamb, lift your head,
> Though the stoniest path you tread,
> Over the mountains lonely,
> Still your bells follow only.

> " Oh, my pet lamb, walk with care,
> Lest you spoil all your wool beware,
> Mother must soon be sewing
> Skins for the summer 's going.

> " Oh, my pet lamb, try to grow
> Fat and fine wheresoe'er you go!
> Know you not, little sweeting,
> A spring lamb is dainty eating!"

[1] Adapted to the metre of the original from the translation of Augusta Plesner and S. Rugeley-Powers.

One day in his twentieth year Arne chanced to overhear a conversation between his mother and the wife of the former gard owner; they were disputing about the horse they owned in common.

"I must wait to hear what Arne says," remarked the mother.

"That lazy fellow!" was the reply. "He would like, I dare say, to have the horse go ranging about the woods as he does himself."

The mother was now silent, although before she had been arguing her own case well.

Arne turned as red as fire. It had not occurred to him before that his mother might have to listen to taunting words for his sake, and yet perhaps she had often been obliged to do so. Why had she not told him of this?

He considered the matter well, and now it struck him that his mother scarcely ever talked with him. But neither did he talk with her. With whom did he talk, after all?

Often on Sunday, when he sat quietly at home, he felt a desire to read sermons to his mother, whose eyes were poor; she had wept too much in her day. But he did not have the courage to do so. Many times he had wanted to offer to read aloud to her from his own books. when all was still in the house. and he

thought the time must hang heavily on her
hands. But his courage failed him for this
too.

"It cannot matter much. I must give up
tending the herds, and move down to mother."

He let several days pass, and became firm
in his resolve. Then he drove the cattle far
around in the wood, and made the following
song : —

"The vale is full of trouble, but here sweet Peace may reign ;
    Within this quiet forest no bailiffs may distrain ;
    None fight, as in the vale, in the Blessed Church's name,
    Yet if a church were here, it would no doubt be just the same.

"How peaceful is the forest : — true, the hawk is far from kind,
    I fear he now is striving the plumpest sparrow to find ;
    I fear yon eagle 's coming to rob the kid of breath,
    And yet perchance if long it lived, it might be tired to death.

"The woodman fells one tree, and another rots away,
    The red fox killed the lambkin white at sunset yesterday ;
    The wolf, though, killed the fox, and the wolf itself must die,
    For Arne shot him down to-day before the dew was dry.

"I 'll hie me to the valley back — the forest is as bad ;
    And I must see to take good heed, lest thinking drive me mad.
    I saw a boy in my dreams, though where I cannot tell —
    But I know he had killed his father — I think it was in Hell." [1]

He came home and told his mother that she
might send out in the parish after another
herd-boy ; he wanted to manage the gard himself. Thus it was arranged ; but the mother

[1] Adapted to the metre of the original, from the translation o
Augusta Plesner and S. Rugeley-Powers.

was always after him with warnings not to overtax himself with work. She used also to prepare such good meals for him at this time that he often felt ashamed; but he said nothing.

He was working at a song, the refrain of which was " Over the lofty mountains." He never succeeded in finishing it, and this was chiefly because he wanted to have the refrain in every other line; finally he gave it up.

But many of the songs he made got out among the people, where they were well liked; there were those who wished very much to talk with him, especially as they had known him from boyhood up. But Arne was shy of all whom he did not know, and thought ill of them, chiefly because he believed they thought ill of him.

His constant companion in the fields was a middle-aged man, called Upland Knut, who had a habit of singing over his work; but he always sang the same song. After listening to this for a few months, Arne was moved to ask him if he did not know any others.

" No," was the man's reply.

Then after the lapse of several days, once when Knut was singing his song, Arne asked:

" How did you chance to learn this *one?* "

" Oh, it just happened so," said the man.

Arne went straight from him into the house ; but there sat his mother weeping, a sight he had not seen since his father's death. He pretended not to notice her, and went toward the door again ; but he felt his mother looking sorrowfully after him again and he had to stop.

" What are you crying for, mother ? "

For a while his words were the only sound in the room, and therefore they came back to him again and again, so often that he felt they had not been said gently enough. He asked once more : —

" What are you crying for ? "

" Oh, I am sure I do not know ; " but now she wept harder than ever.

He waited a long time, then was forced to say, as courageously as he could : —

" There must be something you are crying about ! "

Again there was silence. He felt very guilty, although *she* had said nothing, and *he* knew nothing.

" It just happened so," said the mother. Presently she added, " I am after all most fortunate," and then she wept.

But Arne hastened out, and he felt drawn toward the Kamp gorge. He sat down to look into it, and while he was sitting there, he too wept. "If I only knew what I was crying for," mused Arne.

Above him, in the new-plowed field, Upland Knut was singing his song : —

"Ingerid Sletten of Willow-pool
    Had no costly trinkets to wear;
    But a cap she had that was far more fair,
Although it was only of wool.

"It had no trimming, and now was old,
    But her mother who long had gone
    Had given it her, and so it shone
To Ingerid more than gold.

"For twenty years she laid it aside,
    That it might not be worn away;
    'My cap I'll wear on that blissful day
When I shall become a bride.'

"For thirty years she laid it aside
    Lest the colors might fade away.
    'My cap I'll wear when to God I pray
A happy and grateful bride.'

"For forty years she laid it aside,
    Still holding her mother as dear ;
    'My little cap, I certainly fear
I never shall be a bride.'

"She went to look for the cap one day
    In the chest where it long had lain ;
    But ah! her looking was all in vain, —
The cap had moldered away." [1]

Arne sat and listened as though the words had been music far away up the slope. He went up to Knut.

[1] Translated by Augusta Plesner and S. Rugeley-Powers.

" Have you a mother? " asked he.

" No."

" Have you a father? "

" Oh, no; I have no father."

" Is it long since they died? "

" Oh, yes; it is long since."

" You have not many, I dare say, who care for you? "

" Oh, no; not many."

" Have you any one here? "

" No, not here."

" But yonder in your native parish? "

" Oh, no; not there either."

" Have you not any one at all who cares for you? "

" Oh, no; I have not."

But Arne went from him loving his own mother so intensely that it seemed as though his heart would break; and he felt, as it were, a blissful light over him. " Thou Heavenly Father," thought he, " Thou hast given her to me, and such unspeakable love with the gift, and I put this away from me; and one day when I want it, she will be perhaps no more! " He felt a desire to go to her, if for nothing else only to look at her. But on the way, it suddenly occurred to him : " Perhaps because you did not appreciate her you may soon have

to endure the grief of losing her!" He stood
still at once. "Almighty God! what then
would become of me?"

He felt as though some calamity must be
happening at home. He hastened toward the
house; cold sweat stood on his brow; his feet
scarcely touched the ground. He tore open
the passage door, but within the whole atmos-
phere was at once filled with peace. He softly
opened the door into the family-room. The
mother had gone to bed, the moon shone full in
in her face, and she lay sleeping calmly as a
child.

CHAPTER VI.

Some days after this, mother and son, who of late had been more together, agreed to be present at the wedding of some relatives at a neighboring gard. The mother had not been to any party since she was a girl.

They knew few people at the wedding, save by name, and Arne thought it especially strange that everybody stared at him wherever he went.

Once some words were spoken behind him in the passage; he was not sure, but he fancied he understood them, and every drop of blood rushed into his face whenever he thought of them.

He could not keep his eyes off the man who had spoken these words; finally, he took a seat beside him. But as he drew up to the table he thought the conversation took another turn.

" Well, now I am going to tell you a story, which proves that nothing can be buried so deep down in night that it will not find its way into daylight," said the man, and Arne was sure he looked at *him*. He was an ill-favored man, with thin, red hair encircling a great, round brow. Beneath were a pair of very small eyes and a little bottle-shaped nose; but the mouth was very large, with very pale, out-turned lips. When he laughed, he showed his gums. His hands lay on the table: they were clumsy and coarse, but the wrists were slender. He looked sharp and talked fast, but with much effort. People nicknamed him the Rattle-tongue, and Arne knew that tailor Nils had dealt roughly with him in the old days.

"Yes, there is a great deal of wickedness in this world; it comes nearer home to us than we think. But no matter; you shall hear now of an ugly deed. Those who are old remember Alf, Scrip Alf. 'Sure to come back!' said Alf; that saying comes from him; for when he had struck a bargain — and he could trade, that fellow! — he flung his scrip on his back. 'Sure to come back,' said Alf. A devilish good fellow, fine fellow, splendid fellow, this Alf, Scrip Alf!

"Well, there was Alf and Big Lazy-bones — aye, you knew Big Lazy-bones? — he was big and he was lazy too. He looked too long at a shining black horse Scrip Alf drove and had trained to spring like a summer frog. And before Big Lazy-bones knew what he was

about, he had given fifty dollars for the nag
Big Lazy-bones mounted a carriole,[1] as large as
life, to drive like a king with his fifty-dollar
horse; but now he might lash and swear until
the gard was all in a smoke; the horse ran, for
all that, against all the doors and walls that
were in the way; he was stone blind.

"Afterwards, Alf and Big Lazy-bones fell to
quarreling about this horse all through the parish, just like a couple of dogs. Big Lazy-bones
wanted his money back; but you may believe
he never got so much as two Danish shillings.
Scrip Alf thrashed him until the hair flew.
'Sure to come back,' said Alf. Devilish good
fellow, fine fellow, splendid fellow, this Alf —
Scrip Alf.

"Well, then, some years passed by without
his being heard of again.

"It might have been ten years later that he
was published on the church hill;[2] there had
been left to him a tremendous fortune. Big
Lazy-bones was standing by. 'I knew very
well,' said he, 'that it was money that was crying for Scrip Alf, and not people.'

"Now there was a great deal of gossip about
Alf; and out of it all was gathered that he had

[1] A kind of road-sulky used by travelers in Norway.
[2] Important announcements are made to the people in front
of the church after service.

been seen last on this side of Rören, and not on
the other. Yes, you remember the Rören road
— the old road ?

But Big Lazy-bones had succeeded in rising
to great power and splendor, owning both farm
and complete outfit.

Moreover, he had professed great piety, and
everybody knew he did not become pious for
nothing — any more than other folks do. People began to talk about it.

It was at this time that the Rören road was
to be changed, old-time folks wanted to go
straight ahead, and so it went directly over
Rören ; but we like things level, and so the
road now runs down by the river. There was
a mining and a blasting, until one might have
expected Rören to come tumbling down. All
sorts of officials came there, but the amtmand [1]
oftenest of all, for he was allowed double mile-
age. And now, one day while they were digging down among the rocks, some one went to
pick up a stone, but got hold of a hand that
was sticking out of the rocks, and so strong was
this hand that it sent the man who took hold of
it reeling backwards. Now he who found this
hand was Big Lazy-bones. The lensmand [2]

[1] The chief magistrate of an amt or county.
[2] Bailiff.

was sauntering about there, he was called, and
the skeleton of a whole man was dug out. The
doctor was sent for too; he put the bones so
skillfully together that now only the flesh was
wanting. But people claimed that this skeleton was precisely the same size as Scrip Alf.
'Sure to come back!' said Alf.

"Every one thought it most strange that a
dead hand could upset a fellow like Big Lazy-
bones, even when it did not strike at all. The
lensmand talked seriously to him about it, — of
course when no one was by to hear. But then
Big Lazy-bones swore until everything grew
black about the lensmand.

"'Well, well,' said the lensmand, 'if you
had nothing to do with this, you are just the
fellow to go to bed with the skeleton to-night;
hey?' 'To be sure I am,' replied Big Lazy-
bones. And now the doctor jointed the bones
firmly together, and placed the skeleton in one
of the beds of the barracks. In the other Big
Lazy-bones was to sleep, but the lensmand laid
down in his gown, close up to the wall. When
it grew dark and Big Lazy-bones had to go in
to his bed-fellow, it just seemed as though the
door shut of itself, and he stood in the dark.
But Big Lazy-bones fell to singing hymns, for
he had a strong voice. 'Why are you singing

hymns?' asked the lensmand, outside of the wall. 'No one knows whether he has had the chorister,' answered Big Lazy-bones. Afterward he fell to praying with all his might. 'Why are you praying?' asked the lensmand, outside of the wall. 'He has no doubt been a great sinner,' answered Big Lazy-bones. Then for a long time all was still, and it really seemed as though the lensmand must be sleeping. Then there was a shriek that made the barracks shake. 'Sure to come back!' An infernal noise and uproar arose: 'Hand over those fifty dollars of mine!' bellowed Big Lazy-bones, and there followed a screaming and a wrestling; the lensmand flung open the door, people rushed in with sticks and stones, and there lay Big Lazy-bones in the middle of the floor, and on him was the skeleton."

It was very still around the table. Finally a man who was about to light his clay pipe, said: —

"He surely went mad after that day."

"He did."

Arne felt every one looking at him, and therefore he could not raise his eyes.

"It is, as I have said," put in the first speaker; "nothing can be buried so deep down in night that it will not find its way into daylight!"

"Well, now I will tell about a son who beat his own father," said a fair, heavily-built man, with a round face. Arne knew not where he was sitting.

"It was a bully of a powerful race, over in Hardanger; he was the ruin of many people. His father and he disagreed about the yearly allowance, and the result of this was that the man had no peace at home or in the parish.

"Owing to this he grew more and more wicked, and his father took him to task. 'I will take rebuke from no one,' said the son. 'From me you shall take it as long as I live,' said the father. 'If you do not hold your tongue I will beat you,' said the son, and sprang to his feet. 'Aye, do so if you dare, and you will never prosper in the world,' answered the father, as he too rose. 'Do you think so?'— and the son rushed at him and knocked him down. But the father did not resist; he crossed his arms and let his son do as he chose with him.

"The son beat him, seized hold of him and dragged him to the door. 'I will have peace in the house!' But when they came to the door, the father raised himself up. 'Not farther than to the door,' said he, 'for so far I dragged my own father.' The son paid no heed to this, but dragged his head across the threshold. 'Not farther than to the door, I say!' Here the old man flung his son down at his feet, and chastised him, just as though he were a child."

"That was badly done," said several.

"Did not strike his father, though," Arne thought some one said; but he was not sure of it.

"Now I shall tell *you* something," said Arne, rising up, as pale as death, not knowing what he was going to say. He only saw the words floating about him like great snow-flakes. "I will make a grasp at them hap-hazard!" and he began.

"A troll met a boy who was walking along a road crying. 'Of whom are you most afraid?' said the troll, 'of yourself, or of others?' But the boy was crying, because he had dreamed in the night that he had been forced to kill his wicked father, and so he answered, 'I am most afraid of myself.' 'Then be at peace with yourself, and never cry any more; for hereafter you shall only be at war with others.' And the troll went his way. But the first person the boy met laughed at him,

and so the boy had to laugh back again. The
next person he met struck him; the boy had
to defend himself, and struck back. The third
person he met tried to kill him, and so the boy
had to take his life. Then everybody said
hard things about him, and therefore he knew
only hard things to say of everybody. They
locked their cupboards and doors against him,
so he had to steal his way to what he needed;
he even had to steal his night's rest. Since
they would not let him do anything good, he
had to do something bad. Then the parish
said, 'We must get rid of this boy; he is
so bad; and one fine day they put him out of
the way. But the boy had not the least idea
that he had done anything wicked, and so after
death he came strolling right into the presence
of the Lord. There on a bench sat the father
he had not slain, and right opposite, on another
bench, sat all those who had forced him to do
wrong.

" ' Which bench are you afraid of?' asked
the Lord, and the boy pointed to the long one.

" ' Sit down there, beside your father,' said
the Lord, and the boy turned to do so.

" Then the father fell from the bench, with
a great gash in his neck. In his place there
came one in the likeness of the boy, with re-

pentant countenance and ghastly features; then
another with drunken face and drooping form;
still another with the face of a madman, with
tattered clothes and with hideous laughter.

" ' Thus it might have been with you,' said
the Lord.

" ' Can that really be?' replied the boy,
touching the hem of the Lord's garment.

" Then both benches fell down from heaven,
and the boy stood beside the Lord again and
laughed.

" ' Remember this when you awaken,' said
the Lord, and at that moment the boy awoke.

" Now the boy who dreamed thus is I, and
they who tempted him by thinking him wicked
are you. I no longer fear myself, but I am
afraid of you. Do not stir up my evil pas-
sions, for it is doubtful whether I may get hold
of the Lord's garment.

He rushed out, and the men looked at each
other.

CHAPTER VII.

It was the next day, in the barn of the same gard. Arne had been drunk for the first time in his life, was ill in consequence of it, and had been lying in the barn almost twenty-four hours. Now, turning over, he had propped himself up on his elbows, and thus talked with himself : —

"Everything I look at becomes cowardice. That I did not run away when I was a boy, was cowardice; that I listened to father rather than to mother, was cowardice; that I sang those wicked songs for him was cowardice; I became a herd-boy, that was from cowardice; — I took to reading — oh, yes! that was from cowardice, too; I wanted to hide away from myself. Even after I was grown up, I did not help mother against father — cowardice; that I did not that night — ugh! — cowardice! I should most likely have waited until *she* was killed. I could not stand it at home after that — cowardice; neither did I go my way — cowardice; I did nothing, I tended cattle — cow-

ardice. To be sure, I had promised mother to
stay with her; but I should actually have been
cowardly enough to break the promise, had I
not been afraid to mingle with people. For I
am afraid of people chiefly because I believe
they see how bad I am. And it is fear of people makes me speak ill of them — cursed cowardice! I make rhymes from cowardice. I
dare not think in a straightforward manner
about my own affairs, and so I turn to those
of others — and that is to be a poet.

"I should have sat down and cried until the
hills were turned into water, that is what I
should have done; but instead I say: 'Hush,
hush!' and set myself to rocking. And even
my songs are cowardly; for were they cour-
ageous they would be better. I am afraid of
strong thoughts; afraid of everything that is
strong; if I do rise up to strength, it is in a
frenzy, and frenzy is cowardice. I am more
clever, more capable, better informed than I
seem to be. I am better than my words; but
through cowardice I dare not be what I am.
Fy! I drank brandy from cowardice; I wanted
to deaden the pain! Fy! it hurt. I drank,
nevertheless; drank, nevertheless; drank my
father's heart's blood, and yet I drank! The
fact is, my cowardice is beyond all bounds;

but the most cowardly thing of all is that I can
sit here and say all this to myself.

"Kill myself? Pooh! For that I am too
cowardly. And then I believe in God, — yes,
I believe in God. I long to go to Him; but
cowardice keeps me from Him. From so great
a change a cowardly person winces. But what
if I tried as well as I am able? Almighty
God! What if I tried? I might find a cure
that even my milksop nature could bear; for
I have no bone in me any longer, nor gristle;
only something fluid, slush. . . . . What if I
tried, with good, mild books, — I am afraid
of the strong ones, — with pleasant stories and
legends, all such as are mild; and then a sermon every Sunday and a prayer every evening,
and regular work, that religion may find fruitful soil; it cannot do so amid slothfulness.
What if I tried, dear, gentle God of my
childhood, — what if I tried?"

But some one opened the barn-door, and
hurried across the floor, pale as death, although
drops of sweat rolled down the face. It was
Arne's mother. It was the second day she had
been seeking for her son. She called his name
but did not pause to listen; only called and
rushed about, till he answered from the hay-
mow, where he was lying. She gave a loud

shriek, sprang to the mow more lightly than
a boy, and threw herself upon him.

"Arne, Arne, are you here? So I have
really found you. I have been looking for you
since yesterday; I have searched the whole
night! Poor, poor Arne! I saw they had
wounded you. I wanted so much to talk with
you and comfort you; but then I never dare
talk with you! Arne, I saw you drink! O
God Almighty! let me never see it again!"

It was long before she could say more. "Jesus have mercy on you, my child; I saw you
drink! Suddenly you were gone, drunk and
crushed with grief as you were, and I ran
around to all the houses. I went far out in the
field; I did not find you. I searched in every
copse; I asked every one. I was *here*, too, but
you did not answer me — Arne, Arne! I
walked along the river; but it did not seem to
be deep enough anywhere" — She pressed up
close to him. "Then it came with such relief
to my mind that you might have gone home,
and I am sure I was not more than a quarter of
an hour getting over the road. I opened the
door and looked in every room, and then first
remembered that I myself had the key; you
could not possibly have entered. Arne, last
night I searched along the road on both sides;

I dared not go to the Kamp gorge. I know
not how I came here; no one helped me; but
the Lord put it into my heart that you must
be here!"

He tried to soothe her.

"Arne, indeed, you must never drink brandy
again."

"No, you may be sure of that."

"They must have been very rough with you.
Were they rough with you?"

"Oh, no; it was I who was *cowardly.*" He
laid stress on the word.

"I cannot exactly understand why they
should be rough with you. What was it they
did to you? You will never tell me anything,"
and she began to weep again.

"You never tell me anything, either," said
Arne, gently.

"But you are most to blame, Arne. I got
so into the habit of being silent in your father's
day that you ought to have helped me a little
on the way! My God! there are only two of
us, and we have suffered so much together!"

"Let us see if we cannot do better," whispered Arne. "Next Sunday I will read the
sermon to you."

"God bless you for that! Arne?"

"Yes?"

"I have something I ought to say to you."

"Say it, mother."

"I have sinned greatly against you.; I have done something wrong."

"You, mother?" And it touched him so deeply that his own good, infinitely patient mother should accuse herself of having sinned against him, who had never been really good to her, that he put his arm round her, patted her, and burst into tears.

"Yes, I have; and yet I could not help it."

"Oh, you have never wronged me in any way."

"Yes, I have, — God knows it; it was only because I was so fond of you. But you must forgive me; do you hear?"

"Yes, I will forgive you."

"Well, then, I will tell you about it anotner time; but you will forgive me?"

"Oh, yes, mother!"

"You see, it is perhaps because of this that it has been so hard to talk with you; I have sinned against you."

"I beg of you not to talk so, mother."

"I am happy now, having been able to say so much."

"We must talk more together, we two, mother."

"Yes, that we must; and then you will really read the sermon for me?"

"Yes, I will do so."

"Poor Arne! God bless you!"

"I think it is best for us to go home."

"Yes, we will go home."

"Why are you looking round so, mother?"

"Your father lay in this barn, and wept."

"Father?" said Arne, and grew very pale.

"Poor Nils! It was the day you were christened. Why are you looking round, Arne?"

CHAPTER VIII.

FROM the day that Arne tried with his whole heart to live closer to his mother his relations with other people were entirely changed. He looked on them more with the mother's mild eyes. But he often found it hard to keep true to his resolve; for what he thought most deeply about his mother did not always understand. Here is a song from those days:—

> "It was such a pleasant, sunny day,
>   In-doors I could not think of staying:
> I strolled to the wood, on my back I lay,
>   And rocked what my mind was saying;
> But there crawled emmets, and gnats stung there,
> The wasps and the clegs brought dire despair.

"'My dear, will you not go out in this pleasant weather?' said mother. She sat singing on the porch.

> "It was such a pleasant, sunny day,
>   In-doors I could not think of staying:
> I strayed to a field, on my back I lay,
>   And sang what my mind was saying;
> But snakes came out to enjoy the sun,
> Three ells were they long, and away I run.

"'In such pleasant weather we can go bare-

foot,' said mother, and she pulled off her stock-
ings.

> " It was such a pleasant, sunny day,
>   In-doors I could no longer tarry:
> I stepped in a boat, on my back I lay,
>   The tide did me onward carry;
> The sun, though, scorched till my nose was burned;
> There 's limit to all, so to shore I turned.

" ' What fine days these are for drying the
hay !' said mother, as she shook it with a rake.

> " It was such a pleasant, sunny day,
>   In-doors I could not think of staying:
> I climbed up a tree, and thought there I 'd stay,
>   For there were cool breezes playing.
> A grub to fall on my neck then there chanced;
> I sprang down and screamed, and how madly I danced.

" ' Well, if the cow does not thrive such a day
as this, she never will,' said mother, as she
gazed up the slope.

> " It was such a pleasant, sunny day,
>   In-doors I could no peace discover:
> I made for the force that did loudly play,
>   For *there* it must surely hover;
> But there I drowned while the sun still shone.
> If you made this song, it is surely not my own.[1]

" ' It would take only about three such sunny
days to get everything under cover,' said mother ; and off she started to make my bed."

Nevertheless, this companionship with his

[1] Auber Forestier's translation.

mother brought every day more and more comfort to Arne. What she did not understand
formed quite as much of a tie between them as
what she did understand. For the fact of her
not comprehending a thing made him think it
over oftener, and she grew only the dearer to
him because he found her limits on every side.
Yes, she became infinitely dear to him.

As a child, Arne had not cared much for
nursery stories. Now, as a grown person, he
longed for them, and they led to traditions and
ancient ballads. His mind was filled with a
wonderful yearning; he walked much alone,
and many of the places round about, which for-
merly he had not noticed, seemed strangely
beautiful. In the days when he had gone with
those of his own age to the priest's to prepare
for confirmation, he had often played with them
by a large lake below the parsonage, called
Black Water, because it was deep and black.
He began to think of this lake now, and one
evening he wended his way thither.

He sat down behind a copse, just at the foot
of the parsonage. This lay on the side of a very
steep hill, which towered up beyond until it
became a high mountain; the opposite bank
was similar, and therefore huge shadows were
cast over the lake from both sides, but in its

centre was a stripe of beautiful silvery water.
All was at rest; the sun was just setting; a
faint sound of tinkling bells floated over from
the opposite shore; otherwise profound silence
reigned. Arne did not look right across the
lake, but first turned his eyes toward its lower
end, for there the sun was shedding a sprink-
ling of burning red, ere it departed. Down there
the mountains had parted to make room between them for a long, low valley, and against
this the waves dashed; and it seemed as though
the mountains had gradually sloped together to
form a swing in which to rock this valley, which
was dotted with its many gards. The curling
smoke rose upward, and passed from sight; the
fields were green and reeking; boats laden with
hay were approaching the landings. Arne saw
many people passing to and fro, but could
hear no noise. Thence the eye wandered beyond the shore, where God's dark forest alone
loomed up. Through the forest and along the
lake men had drawn a road, as it were, with
a finger, for a winding streak of dust plainly
marked its course. This Arne's eye followed
until it came directly opposite to where he was
sitting; there the forest ended; the mountains
made a little more room, and straightways gard
after gard lay spread about. The houses were

still larger than those at the lower end, were
painted red, and had higher windows, which
now were in a blaze of light. The hills sparkled
in dazzling sunshine; the smallest child playing
about could be plainly seen; glittering white
sand lay dry on the shore, and upon this little
children bounded with their dogs. But suddenly the whole scene became desolate and
gloomy; the houses dark red, the meadows
dingy green, the sand grayish-white, and the
children small clumps: a mass of mist had
risen above the mountains, and had shut out
the sun. Arne kept his eye fixed on the lake;
there he found everything again. The fields
were rocking there, and the forest silently
joined them; the houses stood looking down,
doors open, and children going out and in.
Nursery tales and childish things came throng-
ing into his mind, as little fish come after a
bait, swim away, come back again, but do not
nibble.

"Let us sit down here until your mother
comes; the priest's lady will surely get through
some time."

Arne was startled; some one had sat down
just behind him.

"But I might be allowed to stay just this one
night," said a beseeching voice, choked with

6

tears; it seemed to be that of a young girl, not quite grown up.

"Do not cry any more; it is shocking to cry because you must go home to your mother." This last came in a mild voice that spoke slowly and belonged to a man.

"That is not the reason I am crying."

"Why are you crying, then?"

"Because I shall no longer be with Mathilde."

This was the name of the priest's only daughter, and reminded Arne that a peasant girl had been brought up with her.

"That could not last forever, any way."

"Yes, but just one day longer, dear!" and she sobbed violently.

"It is best you should go home at once; perhaps it is already too late."

"Too late? Why so? Who ever heard of such a thing?"

"You are peasant-born, and a peasant you shall remain; we cannot afford to keep a fine lady."

"I should still be a peasant, even if I remained here."

"You are no judge of that."

"I have always worn peasant's clothes."

"It is not that which makes the difference."

"I have been spinning and weaving and cooking."

"It is not *that*, either."

"I can talk just as you and mother do."

"Not that, either."

"Then I do not know what it can be," said the girl, and laughed.

"Time will show. Besides, I am afraid you already have too many ideas."

"Ideas, ideas! You are always saying that. I have no ideas." She wept again.

"Oh, you are a weathercock, — that you are!"

"The priest never said so."

"No, but now *I* say so."

"A weathercock? Who ever heard of such a thing? I will not be a weathercock."

"Come, then, what will you be?"

"What will I be? Did you ever hear the like? I will be nothing."

"Very good, then; be nothing."

Now the girl laughed. Presently she said, gravely, "It is unkind of you to say I am nothing."

"Dear me, when that was what you wanted to be yourself!"

"No, I do not want to be nothing."

"Very good, then; be everything."

The girl laughed. Presently, with a sorrowful voice, " The priest never fooled with me in this way."

" No, he only made a fool of you."

" The priest? You have never been so kind to me as the priest has."

" No, for that would have spoiled you."

" Sour milk can never become sweet."

" Oh, yes, when it is boiled to whey."

Here the girl burst out laughing.

" There comes your mother."

Then she grew sober again.

" Such a long-winded woman as the priest's lady I have never met in all the days of my life," here interposed a shrill, rattling voice. " Make haste, now, Baard. Get up and push the boat out. We will not get home to-night. The lady wished me to see that Eli kept her feet dry. Dear me, you will have to see to that yourself. Every morning she must take a walk, for the sake of her health. It is health, health, from morning till night. Get up, now, Baard, and push out the boat. Just think, I have to set sponge this evening ! "

" The chest has not come yet," said he, and lay still.

" But the chest is not to come, either; it is

to remain until the first Sunday there is service. Do you hear, Eli? Pick yourself up; take your bundle, and come. Get up, now, Baard!"

She led the way, and the girl followed.

" Come, now, I say, — come now!" resounded from below.

" Have you looked after the plug in the boat?" asked Baard, still without rising.

" Yes, it is there;" and Arne heard her just then hammering it in with the scoop. "But get up, I say, Baard! Surely we are not to stay here all night?"

" I am waiting for the chest."

" But, my dear, bless you, I have told you it is to wait until the first Sunday there is service."

" There it comes," said Baard, and they heard the rattling of a cart.

" Why, I said it was to wait until the first Sunday there is service."

" I said we were to take it along."

Without anything further, the wife hastened up to the cart, and carried the bundle, the lunch-box, and other small things down to the boat. Then Baard arose, went up, and took the chest himself.

But behind the cart there came rushing along

a girl in a straw hat, with floating hair; it was the priest's daughter.

"Eli! Eli!" she called, as she ran.

"Mathilde! Mathilde!" Eli answered, and ran toward her.

They met on the hill, put their arms about each other, and wept. Then Mathilde took up something she had set down on the grass: it was a bird-cage.

"You shall have Narrifas; yes, you shall. Mother wishes it, too. You shall, after all, have Narrifas, — indeed, you shall; and then you will think of 'me. And very often row — row — row over to me," and the tears of both flowed freely.

"Eli! Come, now, Eli! Do not stand there!" was heard from below.

"But I want to go along," said Mathilde. "I want to go and sleep with you to-night!"

"Yes, yes, yes!" and with arms twined about each other's necks they moved down toward the landing.

Presently Arne saw the boat out on the water. Eli stood high on the stern, with the bird-cage, and waved her hand; Mathilde was left behind, and sat on the stone landing weeping.

She remained sitting there as long as the

boat was on the water; it was but a short distance across to the red house, as said before;
and Arne kept his seat, too. He watched the
boat, as she did. It soon passed into the darkness, and he waited until it drew up to the
shore: then he saw Eli and her parents in the
water; in it he followed them up toward the
houses, until they came to the prettiest one of
them all. He saw the mother go in first, then
the father with the chest, and last of all the
daughter, so far as he could judge from their
size. Soon after the daughter came out again,
and sat down in front of the store-house door,
probably that she might gaze over at the other
side, where at that moment the sun was shedding its parting rays. But the young lady
from the parsonage had already gone, and Arne
alone sat watching Eli in the water.

"I wonder if she sees me!"

He got up and moved away. The sun had
set, but the sky was bright and clear blue, as it
often is of a summer night. Mist from land
and water rose and floated over the mountains
on both sides; but the peaks held themselves
above it, and stood peering at one another.
He went higher up. The lake grew blacker and
deeper, and seemed, as it were, to contract.
The upper valley shortened, and drew closer to

the lake. The mountains were nearer to the eye,
but looked more like a shapeless mass, for the
light of the sun defines. The sky itself appeared nearer, and all surrounding objects became friendly and familiar.

CHAPTER IX.

LOVE and woman were beginning to play a prominent part in his thoughts; in the ancient ballads and stories of the olden times such themes were reflected as in a magic mirror, just as the girl had been in the lake. He constantly brooded over them, and after that evening he found pleasure in singing about them; for they seemed, as it were, to have come nearer home to him. But the thought glided away, and floated back again with a song that was unknown to him; he felt as though another had made it for him,—

"Fair Venevill bounded on lithesome feet
    Her lover to meet.
He sang till it sounded afar away,
    'Good-day, good-day,'
While blithesome birds were singing on every blooming spray
    'On Midsummer Day
    There is dancing and play;
But now I know not whether she weaves her wreath or nay.'

"She wove him a wreath of corn-flowers blue:
    'Mine eyes so true.'
He took it, but soon away it was flung:
    'Farewell!' he sung;
And still with merry singing across the fields he sprung.
    'On Midsummer Day,' etc.

" She wove him a chain.   ' Oh, keep it with care!
    'T is made of my hair.'
She yielded him then, in an hour of bliss,
    Her pure first kiss ;
But he blushed as deeply as she the while her lips met his.
    ' On Midsummer Day,' etc.

" She wove him a wreath with a lily-band :
    ' My true right hand.'
She wove him another with roses aglow :
    ' My left hand, now.'
He took them gently from her, but blushes dyed his brow
    ' On Midsummer Day,' etc.

" She wove him a wreath of all flowers round :
    ' All I have found.'
She wept, but she gathered and wove on still :
    ' Take all you will.'
Without a word he took it, and fled across the hill.
    ' On Midsummer Day,' etc.

" She wove on, bewildered and out of breath :
    ' My bridal wreath.'
She wove till her fingers aweary had grown :
    ' Now put it on.'
But when she turned to see him, she found that he had gone.
    ' On Midsummer Day,' etc.

" She wove on in haste, as for life and death,
    Her bridal wreath ;
But the Midsummer sun no longer shone,
    And the flowers were gone ;
But though she had no flowers, wild fancy still wove on.
    ' On Midsummer-Day
    There is dancing and play ;
But now I know not whether she weaves her wreath or nay."

[1] Translated by Augusta Plesner and S. Rugeley-Powers.

It was his own intense melancholy that called forth the first image of love that glided so gloomily through his soul. A twofold longing, — to have some one to love and to become something great, — blended together and became one. At this time he was working again at the song, "Over the lofty mountains," altering it, and all the while singing and thinking quietly to himself, "Surely I will get 'over' some day; I will sing until I gain courage." He did not forget his mother in these his thoughts of roving; indeed, he took comfort in the thought that as soon as he got firm foothold in the strange land, he would come back after her, and offer her conditions which he never could be able to provide for her at home. But in the midst of all these mighty yearnings there played something calm, cheering, refined, that darted away and came again, took hold and fled, and, dreamer that he had become, he was more in the power of these spontaneous thoughts than he himself was aware.

There lived in the parish a jovial man whose name was Ejnar Aasen. When he was twenty years old he had broken his leg; since then he had walked with a cane; but wherever he came hobbling along, there was always mirth

afoot. The man was rich. On his property
there was a large nut-wood, and there was sure
to be assembled, on one of the brightest, pleas-
antest days in autumn, a group of merry girls
gathering nuts. At these nutting-parties he
had plenty of feasting for his guests all day,
and dancing in the evening. For most of
these girls he had been godfather; indeed, he
was the godfather of half the parish; all the
children called him godfather, and from them
every one else, both old and young, learned
to do so.

Godfather and Arne were well acquainted,
and he liked the young man because of the
verses he made. Now godfather asked Arne to
come to the nutting-party. Arne blushed and
declined; he was not used to being with girls,
he said.

"Then you must get used to it," replied
godfather.

Arne could not sleep at night because of
this; fear and yearning were at war within
him; but whatever the result might be, he
went along, and was about the only youth
among all these girls. He could not deny that
he felt disappointed; they were neither those
he had sung about, nor those he had feared
to meet. There was an excitement and mer-

riment, the like of which he had never known
before, and the first thing that struck him was
that they could laugh over nothing in the
world; and if three laughed, why, then, five
laughed, simply because those three laughed.
They all acted as though they were members
of the same household; and yet many of them
had not met before that day. If they caught
the bough they were jumping after, they
laughed at that, and if they did not catch it,
they laughed at that, too. They fought for
the hook to draw it down with; those who
got it laughed, and those who did not get it,
laughed also. Godfather hobbled after them
with his cane, and offered all the hindrance
in his power. Those whom he caught laughed
because he caught them, and those whom he
did not catch laughed because he did not catch
them. But they all laughed at Arne for being
sober, and when he tried to laugh, they laughed,
because he was laughing at last.

They seated themselves finally on a large hill,
godfather in the centre, and all the girls around
him. The hill commanded a fine outlook; the
sun scorched; but the girls heeded it not, they
sat, casting nut-husks and shells at one another,
giving the kernels to godfather. He tried to
quiet them at last, striking at them with his

cane, as far as he could reach; for now he
wanted them to tell stories, above all, something amusing. But to get them started seemed
more difficult than to stop a carriage on a hill-
side. Godfather began himself. There were
many who did not want to listen; for they
knew already everything he had to tell; but
they all ended by listening attentively. Before they knew what they were about, they sat
in the centre, and each took her turn in following his example as best she could. Now
Arne was much astonished to find that just
in proportion to the noise the girls had made
before was the gravity of the stories they now
told. Love was the chief theme of these.

"But you, Aasa, have a good one; I remember that from last year," said godfather,
turning to a plump girl with a round, pleasant
face, who sat braiding the hair of a younger
sister, whose head was in her lap.

"Several that are here may know that," said
she.

"Well, give it to us anyway," they begged.

"I will not have to be urged long," said
she, and, still braiding, she told and sang, as
follows: —

"There was a grown-up youth who tended
cattle, and he was in the habit of driving his

herds upward, along the banks of a broad
stream. High up on his way, there was a crag
which hung out so far over the stream, that
when he stood on it he could call out to any
one on the other side. For on the other side
of the stream there was a herd-girl whom he
could see all day long, but he could not come
over to her.

> ' Now, tell me thy name, thou girl that art sitting,
> Up there with thy sheep, so busily knitting? '

he asked, over and over again, for many days,
until at last one day there came the answer, —

> ' My name floats about like a duck in wet weather; —
> Come over, thou boy in the cap of brown leather.'

" But this made the youth no wiser than
before, and he thought he would pay no further
heed to the girl. This was not so easy, though,
for, let him drive the cattle where he would,
he was always drawn back to the crag. Then
the youth grew alarmed, and called over : —

> ' Well, who is your father, and where are you biding?
> On the road to the church I have ne'er seen you riding.'

" The youth more than half believed her, in
fact, to be a hulder.[1]

> ' My house is burned down, and my father is drowned,
> And the road to the church-hill I never have found.'

[1] The hulder dwells in forests and mountains, appears like a
beautiful woman, and usually wears a blue petticoat and a white
hood. She has a long tail, which she tries to conceal when she
is among people. She is fond of cattle.

"Now this also made the youth no wiser than before. By day he lingered on the crag, and by night he dreamed that she was dancing around him, and gave him a lash with a great cow's-tail each time he tried to take hold of her. Soon he could not sleep at all, neither could he work, and the poor youth was in a wretched state. Again he called aloud, —

'If thou art a hulder, then pray do not spell me, —
If thou art a maiden, then hasten to tell me?'

"But there came no answer, and then he was sure that this was a hulder. He gave up tending cattle, but it was just as bad, for wherever he went, or whatever he did, he thought of the fair hulder who blew on the horn.

"Then one day, as he stood chopping wood, there came a girl through the yard who actually looked like the hulder. But when she came nearer, it was not she. He thought much about this ; then the girl came back, and in the distance it was the hulder, and he ran directly toward her. But the moment he came near her it was not she.

"After this, let the youth be at church, at a dance, at other social gatherings, or where he would, the girl was there too ; when he was far from her, she seemed to be the hulder near to her, she seemed to be another; he asked her then whether it were she or not; but she laughed at him. It is just as well to spring into it as to creep into it, thought the youth, and so he married the girl.

"No sooner was this done than the youth ceased to like the girl. Away from her, he longed for her; but when with her, he longed for one he did not see; therefore he was harsh toward his wife; she bore this and was silent.

"But one day, when he was searching for the horses, he found his way to the crag, and sitting down, he called out, —

'Like fairy moonlight to me thou seemest,
  Like midsummer fires from afar thou gleamest.'

"He thought it did him good to sit there, and he fell into the way of going thither whenever anything went amiss at home. The wife wept when she was left alone.

"But one day, while the youth was sitting on the crag, the hulder, her living self, appeared on the opposite side, and blew her horn. He eagerly cried, —

'Ah, dear, art thou come! all around thee is shining!
  Ah, blow now again! I am sitting here pining.'

"Then she answered, —

7

'Away from thy mind the dreams I am blowing, —
The rye is all rotting for want of mowing.'

"But the youth was frightened, and went home again. Before long, though, he was so tired of his wife that he felt compelled to wander off to the wood and take his seat on the crag. Then a voice sang, —

'I dreamed thou wast here; ho, hasten to bind me!
No, not over there, but behind you will find me.' [1]

"The youth started up, looked about him, and espied a green skirt disappearing through the woods. He pursued. Now there was a chase through the woods. As fleet of foot as the hulder was, no mortal could be; he cast steel [2] over her again and again; she ran on the same as before. By and by she began to grow tired. The youth knew this from her foot-fall, though her form convinced him that it was the hulder herself, and none other. 'You shall surely be mine now,' thought the youth, and suddenly flung his arms about her with such force that both he and she rolled far down the hill before they could stop. Then the hulder laughed until the youth thought the mountains

[1] Translated by Augusta Plesner and S. Rugeley-Powers.
[2] Shooting or flinging steel over the head of hulders, trolls, etc., makes the witchery vanish. Thus also a piece of steel laid in the cradle prevents hulders from exchanging little children for their own.

fairly rang; he took her on his knee, and she looked so fair, just as he had once thought his wife would look.

"'Oh, dear, who are you that are so fair?' asked the youth, and as he caressed her, he felt that her cheeks were warm and glowing.

"'Why, good gracious, I am your wife,' said she."

The girls laughed, and thought the youth was very foolish. But godfather asked Arne if he had been listening.

"Well, now, I will tell you something," said a little girl, with a little round face, and such a very little nose.

"There was a little youth who wanted very much to woo a little maiden; they were both grown up, yet were both very small indeed. But the youth could not muster up courage enough to begin his wooing. He always joined her after church, but they did not then get beyond the weather in their talk; he sought her at the dances, and he danced her almost to death, but talk with her he could not. 'You must learn to write, and then you will not have to,' said he to himself, and so the youth took to writing; but he never thought he could do well enough, and so he wrote a whole year before he dared think of a letter. Then the

trouble was how to deliver it so that no one
should see, and he waited until once they
chanced to meet alone behind the church.

" ' I have a letter for you,' said the youth.

" ' But I cannot read writing,' answered the
maiden.

" And the youth got no further.

" Then he took service at her father's house,
and hung round her the whole day long. Once
he came very near speaking to her ; he had
already opened his mouth, when there flew
into it a large fly. 'If only no one comes and
takes her from me,' thought the youth. But
there came no one to take her from him, because she was so small.

" Some one did come along, though, at last,
for he was small too. The youth well knew
what he was after, and when he and the girl
went up-stairs together, the youth made his
way to the key-hole. Now he who was within
offered himself. 'Alas, dunce that I am, not
to have made more haste ! ' thought the youth.
He who was inside kissed the girl right on the
lips. 'That must have tasted good,' thought
the youth. But he who was inside had drawn
the girl down on his knee. 'What a world
we live in ! ' said the youth, and wept. This
the girl heard, and went to the door.

" ' What do you want of me, you ugly boy, that you never give me any peace ? '

" ' I ? — I only wanted to ask you if I might be your groomsman.'

" ' No; my brothers are to be the grooms-men,' answered the girl, — and slammed the door in his face.

" And the youth got no further."

The girls laughed a great deal at this story, and sent a shower of husks flying round after it.

Godfather now wanted Eli Böen to tell something.

What should it be ?

Why, she might tell what she had told over on the hill, when he was with them, the time she gave him the new garters. It was a good while before Eli was ready, for she laughed so hard, but at last she told : —

" A girl and a boy were walking together on the same road. ' Why, see the thrush that is following us,' said the girl. ' It is I whom it is following,' said the boy. ' It is just as likely to be me,' answered the girl. ' That we can soon see,' remarked the boy; ' now you take the lower road, and I will take the upper one, and we will meet at the top of the hill.' They did so. ' Was it not following me ? ' asked the boy, when they met. ' No, it was following me,'

answered the girl. ' Then there must be two.'
They walked together again a little way, but
then there was only one thrush ; the boy thought
it flew on his side ; but the girl thought it flew
on hers. ' The deuce ! I 'll not bother my head
any more about that thrush,' said the boy. ' Nor
I either,' replied the girl.

"But no sooner had they said this than the
thrush was gone. ' It was on *your* side,' said
the boy. ' No, I thank you ; I saw plainly it
was on *yours*. But there ! There it comes
again ! ' called out the girl. ' Yes, it is on *my*
side ! ' cried the boy. But now the girl became angry. ' May all the plagues take me if
I walk with you any longer !' and she went her
own way. Then the thrush left the boy, and
the way became so tedious that he began to
call out. She answered. ' Is the thrush with
you ? ' shouted the boy. ' No, it is with you.'
' Oh, dear ! You must come here again, then
perhaps it will come too.' And the girl came
again ; they took each other by the hand and
walked together. ' Kvit, kvit, kvit, kvit !' was
heard on the girl's side. ' Kvit, kvit, kvit,
kvit !' was heard on the boy's side. ' Kvit, kvit,
kvit, kvit, kvit, kvit, kvit, kvit !' was heard on
both sides, and when they came to look, there
were a thousand million thrushes round about

them. ' Why, how strange !' said the girl, and
looked up at the boy. ' Bless you! ' said the
boy, and caressed the girl."

This story all the girls thought fine.

Then godfather suggested that they should
tell what they had dreamed the night before,
and he would decide who had had the finest
dream.

What! tell their dreams? No, indeed!
And there was no end to the laughing and whispering. But then one after another began to
remark that she had had such a fine dream last
night ; others, again, that, fine as the ones they
had had, it could not by any means be. And
finally, they all were seized with a desire to tell
their dreams. But it must not be out loud, it
must only be to *one*, and that must by no
means be godfather. Arne was sitting quietly on the hill, and so he was the one to whom
they dared tell their dreams.

Arne took a seat beneath a hazel, and then
she who had told the first story came to him.
She thought a long time, and then told as follows : —

" I dreamed I stood by a great lake. Then
I saw some one go on the water, and it was
one whom I will not name. He climbed up in
a large pond-lily, and sat and sang. But I

went out on one of those large leaves that the pond-lily has, and which lie and float; on it I wanted to row over to him. But no sooner had I stepped on the leaf than it began to sink with me, and I grew much alarmed and cried. Then he came rowing over to me in the pond-lily, lifted me up to where he sat, and we rowed all over the lake. Was not that a nice dream?"

The little maiden who had told the little story now came.

"I dreamed I had caught a little bird, and I was so happy that I did not want to let it go until I got home. But there I did not dare let go of it, lest father and mother should tell me I must let it out again. So I went up in the garret with it, but there the cat was lurking, and so I could not let go of it there either. Then I did not know what to do, so I took it up in the hay-loft; but, good gracious! there were so many cracks there that it could easily fly away! Well, then I went out in the yard again, and there I thought stood one whom I will not name. He was playing with a large, black dog. 'I would rather play with that bird of yours,' said he, and came close up to me. But I thought I started to run, and he and the large dog after me, and thus I ran all round the yard; but then mother opened

the front door, drew me quickly in, and slammed
the door. Outside, the boy stood laughing,
with his face against the window-pane. 'See,
here is the bird!' said he, — and, just think, he
really had the bird! Was not that a funny
dream?"

Then she came who had told about all the
thrushes, — Eli they had called her. It was
the Eli he had seen that evening in the boat and
in the water. She was the same and yet not
the same, so grown-up and pretty she looked as
she sat there, with her delicately cut face and
slender form. She laughed immoderately, and
therefore it was long before she could control
herself; but then she told as follows:—

"I had been feeling so glad that I was coming to the nutting-party to-day that I dreamed
last night I was sitting here on the hill. The
sun shone brightly, and I had a whole lapful
of nuts. But then there came a little squirrel,
right in among the nuts, and it sat on its hind
legs in my lap and ate them all up. Was not
that a funny dream?"

Yet other dreams were told Arne, and then
he was to decide which was the finest. He
had to take a long time to consider, and meanwhile godfather started off with the whole
crowd for the gard, and Arne was to follow.

They sprang down the hill, formed in a row when they had reached the plain, and sang all the way to the house.

Arne still sat there listening to the singing. The sun fell directly on the group, it shone on their white sleeves; soon they twined their arms about each other's waists; they went dancing across the meadow, godfather after them with his cane, because they were treading down his grass. Arne thought no more about the dreams. Soon he even left off watching the girls; his thoughts wandered far beyond the valley, as did the fine sunbeams, and he sat alone there on the hill and spun. Before he was aware of it, he was entangled in a close web of melancholy; he yearned to break away, and never in the world before so ardently as now. He faithfully promised himself that when he got home he would talk with his mother, come of it what would.

His thoughts grew stronger, and drifted into the song, —

"Over the lofty mountains."

Words had never flowed so readily as now, nor had they ever blended so surely into verse, — they almost seemed like girls sitting around on a hill. He had a scrap of paper about him and placing it on his knee, he wrote. When the song was complete, he arose, like one who was released, felt that he could not see people, and took the forest road home, although he knew that the night, too, would be needed for this. The first time he sat down to rest on the way, he felt for the song, that he might sing it aloud as he went along, and let it be borne all over the parish ; but he found he had left it in the place where it was written.

One of the girls went up the hill to look for him, did not find him, but found his song.

CHAPTER X.

To talk with the mother was more easily thought than done. Arne alluded to Kristian and the letter that never came; but the mother went away from him, and for whole days after he thought her eyes looked red. He had also another indication of her feelings, and that was that she prepared unusually good meals for him.

He had to go up in the woods to fetch an armful of fuel one day; the road led through the forest, and just where he was to do his chopping was the place where people went to pick whortleberries in the autumn. He had put down his axe in order to take off his jacket, and was just about beginning, when two girls came walking along with berry pails. It was his wont to hide himself rather than meet girls, and so he did now.

"O dear, O dear! What a lot of berries! Eli, Eli!"

"Yes, dear, I see them."

"Well, then, do not go any farther; here are many pailfuls!"

"I thought there was a rustling in that bush over there!"

"Oh, you must be mad!" and the girls rushed at each other, and put their arms about each other's waists. They stood for a long while so still, that they scarcely breathed.

"It is surely nothing; let us go on picking!"

"Yes, I really think we will."

And so they began to gather berries.

"It was very kind of you, Eli, to come over to the parsonage to-day. Have you anything to tell me?"

"I have been at godfather's."

"Yes, you told me that; but have you nothing about *him*, — you know who?"

"Oh, yes!"

"Oh, oh! Eli, is that so? Make haste; tell me!"

"He has been there again!"

"Oh, nonsense!"

"Yes, indeed; both father and mother pretended they did not see it, but I went up in the garret and hid."

"More, more! Did he follow you there?"

"I think father told him where I was; he is always so provoking."

"And so he came? Sit down, sit down here beside me. Well, so he came?"

" Yes ; but he did not say much, for he was so bashful."

" Every word ! Do you hear ? every word ! "

" ' Are you afraid of me ? ' said he. ' Why should I be afraid ? ' said I. ' You know what it is I want of you,' said he, and sat down on the chest beside me."

" Beside you ! "

" And then he put his arm round my waist."

" His arm round your waist ? Are you wild ? "

" I wanted to get away from him, but he would not let me go. ' Dear Eli,' said he," — she laughed, and the other girl laughed too.

" Well ? well ? "

" ' Will you be my wife ? ' "

" Ha, ha, ha ! "

" Ha, ha, ha ! "

And then both — " Ha, ha, ha, ha, ha, ha ! "

Finally, the laughter, too, had to come to an end, and then a long silence ensued. After a while, the first one asked, but softly, " Say, — was it not too bad that he put his arm round your waist ? "

Either the other one made no reply to this, or else she spoke in such a low tone that it could not be heard ; perhaps, too, she answered only with a smile. Presently the first one asked : —

" Have neither your father nor your mother said anything since ?"

"Father came up and looked at me, but I kept hiding; for he laughed every time he saw me."

" But your mother? "

" Why, she said nothing; but she was less harsh than usual."

" Well, you certainly refused him ?"

" Of course."

Then there was a long silence again.

"Eli !"

" Well? "

" Do you think any one will ever come that way to me?"

" Yes, to be sure."

" How you talk ! O — h! say, Eli ? What if he should put his arm round my waist?" She covered her face.

There was much laughter, afterwards whispering and tittering.

The girls soon went away. They had neither seen Arne, nor the axe and the jacket, and he was glad.

Some days later he put Upland Knut in the houseman's place under Kampen.

" You shall no longer be lonely," said Arne.

Arne himself took to steady work. He had

early learned to cut with the hand-saw, for he
had himself added much to the house at home.
Now he wanted to work at his trade, for he
knew it was well to have some definite occupa-
tion; it was also good for him to get out among
people; and so changed had he gradually become, that he longed for this whenever he had
kept to himself for a while. Thus it came to
pass that he was at the parsonage for a time
that winter doing carpentering, and the two
girls were often together there. Arne won-
dered, when he saw them, who it could be that
was now courting Eli Böen.

It so happened one day, when they went out
for a ride, that Arne had to drive for the young
lady of the parsonage and Eli; he had good
ears, yet could not hear what they were talking
about; sometimes Mathilde spoke to him, at
which Eli laughed and hid her face. Once
Mathilde asked if it was true he could make
verses. "No!" he said promptly: then they
both laughed, chattered, and laughed. This
made him indignant, and he pretended not to
see them.

Once he was sitting in the servants' hall,
when there was dancing there. Mathilde and
Eli both came in to look on. They were disputing about something in the corner where

they stood. Eli would not, but Mathilde would,
and she won. Then they both crossed the floor
to him, courtesied, and asked whether he could
dance. He answered "No," and then they
both turned, laughed, and ran away. "They
keep up a perpetual laughter," thought Arne,
and became sober. But the priest had a little
adopted son, about ten or twelve years old,
of whom Arne thought a good deal; from this
boy Arne learned to dance when no one else
was present.

Eli had a little brother about the same age
as the priest's adopted son. These two were
playmates, and Arne made sleds, skees,[1] and
snares for them ; and he often talked with them
about their sisters, especially about Eli. One
day Eli's brother brought word that Arne
should not be so careless with his hair.

"Who said so?"

"Eli said so; but I was not to tell that she
said so."

Some days after, Arne sent a message to Eli
that she should laugh a little less. The boy
came back with the reply that Arne should
laugh a little more.

Once the boy asked for something he had
written. Arne let him have it, and thought

[1] A kind of long snow-shoe.

8

no more of it. After a while the boy thought
he would please Arne with the tidings that
both the girls liked his writing very much.

" Why, have they seen it ? "

" Yes, it was for them I wanted it."

Arne asked the boys to bring him something
their sisters had written; they did so. Arne
corrected the mistakes with a carpenter's pen-
cil. He asked the boys to place the paper where
it could easily be found. Afterwards he found
it again in his jacket pocket, but at the bottom was written, " Corrected by a conceited
fellow ! "

The next day Arne finished his work at the
parsonage, and set out for home. So gentle as
he was this winter, his mother had never seen
him since those sorrowful days after his father's
death. He read the sermon for her, went with
her to church, and was very kind to her. But
she well knew it was all to get her consent to
journey away from her when spring came.
Then one day he had a message from Böen to
know if he would come there and do some carpentering.

Arne was quite startled, and answered "Yes."
as though he scarcely knew what he was saying. No sooner had the messenger gone than
the mother said,

"You may well be astonished! From Böen?"

"Is that so strange?" asked Arne, but did not look at her as he spoke.

"From Böen ' cried the mother, once more.

"Well, why not as well from there as from another gard?' Arne now looked up a little.

"From Böen and Birgit Böen! Baard, who gave your father the blow that was his ruin, and that for Birgit Böen's sake!"

"What do you say?" now cried the youth "Was that Baard Böen?"

Son and mother stood and looked at each other. Between the two a whole life was un folded, and this was a moment wherein they could see the black thread which all along had been woven through it. They fell later to talk ing about the father's proud days, when old El Böen herself had courted him for her daughter Birgit, and got a refusal. They went through his whole life just as far as where he was knocked down, and both found out that Baard's fault had been the least. Nevertheless, it was he who had given the father that fatal blow, — he it was.

"Am I not yet done with father?" then thought Arne, and decided at the same mo ment to go.

When Arne came walking, with the hand-

saw on his shoulder, over the ice and up toward
Böen, it seemed to him a pretty gard. The
house always looked as though it were newly
painted; he was a little chilled, and that was
perhaps why it seemed so cozy to him. He did
not go directly in, but went beyond toward the
stable, where a flock of shaggy goats were standing in the snow, gnawing at the bark of some
fir branches. A shepherd dog walked to and
fro on the barn-bridge, and barked as though
the devil himself was coming to the gard; but
the moment Arne stood still, he wagged his tail
and let him pat him. The kitchen door on the
farther side of the house was often opened, and
Arne looked down there each time; but it was
either the dairy-maid, with tubs and pails, or
the cook, who was throwing something out to
the goats. Inside the barn they were thresh-
ing with frequent strokes, and to the left, in
front of the wood-shed, stood a boy chopping
wood; behind him there were many layers of
wood piled up.

Arne put down his saw and went into the
kitchen; there white sand was spread on the
floor, and finely cut juniper leaves strewed over
it; on the walls glittered copper kettles, and
crockery stood in rows. They were cooking
dinner. Arne asked to speak with Baard. "Ge

into the sitting-room," some one said, pointing to the door. He went; there was no latch to the door, but a brass handle; it was cheerful in there, and brightly painted, the ceiling was decorated with many roses, the cupboards were red, with the owner's name in black, the bedstead was also red, but bordered with blue stripes. By the stove sat a broad-shouldered man, with a mild face, and long, yellow hair; he was putting hoops about some pails; by the long table sat a tall, slender woman, with a high linen cap on her head, and dressed in tight-fitting clothes; she was sorting corn into two heaps. Besides these there were no others in the room.

"Good day, and bless the work!" said Arne, drawing off his hat. Both looked up; the man smiled, and asked who it was.

"It is he who is to do carpentering."

The man smiled more, and said, as he nodded his head and began his work again, —

"Well, then, it is Arne Kampen!"

"Arne Kampen?" cried the wife, and stared fixedly before her.

The man looked up hastily, and smiled again. "The son of tailor Nils," he said, and went on once more with his work.

After a while, the wife got up, crossed the

floor to the shelf, turned, went to the cupboard, turned again, and as she at last was rummaging in a table drawer, she asked, without looking up, —

"Is *he* to work *here?*"

"Yes, that he is," said the man, also without looking up. "It seems no one has asked you to sit down," he observed, addressing himself to Arne.

The latter took a seat; the wife left the room, the man continued to work; and so Arne asked if he too should begin.

"Let us first have dinner."

The wife did not come in again; but the next time the kitchen-door opened it was Eli who came. She appeared at first not to notice Arne; when he rose to go to her, she stood still, and half turned to give him her hand, but she did not look at him. They exchanged a few words; the father worked on. Eli had her hair braided, wore a tight-sleeved dress, was slender and straight, had round wrists and small hands. She laid the table; the working-people dined in the next room, but Arne with the family in this one; it so happened that they had their meals separately to-day; usually they all ate at the same table in the large, light kitchen.

"Is not mother coming?" asked the man.

" No, she is up-stairs weighing wool."

" Have you asked her ? "

" Yes; but she says she does not want any-thing."

There was silence for a while.

" But it is cold up-stairs."

" She did not want me to make a fire."

After dinner Arne began work; in the even-ing he was again with the family in the sitting-room. Then the wife, too, was there. The women were sewing. The husband was busy with some trifles, and Arne helped him; there was a prolonged silence, for Eli, who usually led in conversation, was also silent. Arne thought with dismay that it probably was often thus at his own home; but he realized it now for the first time. Eli drew a long breath at last, as though she had restrained herself long enough, and then she fell to laughing. Then the father also laughed, and Arne, too, thought it was laughable, and joined in. From this time forth they talked of various things; but it ended in Arne and Eli doing most of the talking, the fa-ther putting in an occasional word. But once, when Arne had been speaking for some time and happened to look up, he met the eyes of the mother, Birgit; she had dropped her sewing, and sat staring fixedly at him. Now she

picked up her work again, but at the first word
he spoke she raised her eyes.

Bed-time came, and each one went his way.
Arne thought he would notice the dream he
had the first night in a new place; but there
seemed to be no sense in it. The whole day
long he had talked little or none with the master of the gard, but at night it was of him he
dreamed. The last thing was that Baard sat
playing cards with tailor Nils. The latter was
very angry and pale in the face; but Baard
smiled and won the game.

Arne remained several days, during which
time there was scarcely any talking, but a great
deal of work. Not only those in the family
room were silent, but the servants, the tenants,
even the women. There was an old dog on the
gard that barked every time strangers came;
but the gard people never heard the dog without
saying "hush!" and then he went growling off
and laid down again. At home at Kampen
there was a large weather-vane on the house,
which turned with the wind; there was a still
larger vane here, to which Arne's attention was
attracted because it did not turn. When there
was a strong current of wind, the vane strug-
gled to get loose, and Arne looked at it until he
felt compelled to go up on the roof and set the

vane free. It was not frozen fast, as he had
supposed, but a pin was stuck through it that
it might be kept still. This Arne took out and
threw down; the pin struck Baard, who came
walking along. He glanced up.

" What are you doing there ? "

" I am letting loose the vane."

" Do not do so; it makes such a wailing
noise when it is in motion."

Arne sat astride the gable.

" That is better than always being quiet."

Baard looked up at Arne, and Arne looked
down on Baard; then Baard smiled.

" He who has to howl when he talks had
much better keep silent, I am sure."

Now it often happens that words haunt us
long after they were uttered, especially when
they were the last ones heard. So these words
haunted Arne when he crept down in the cold
from the roof, and were still with him in the
evening when he entered the family room. Eli
was standing, in the twilight, by a window, gazing out over the ice which lay glittering beneath the moon's beams. Arne went to the
other window and looked out as she was do
ing. Within all was cozy and quiet, without it
was cold; a sharp wind swept across the valley, so shaking the trees that the shadows they

cast in the moonlight did not lie still, but went
groping about in the snow. From the parsonage
there glimmered a light, opening out and clos-
ing in, assuming many shapes and colors, as
light is apt to do when one gazes at it too
long. The mountain loomed up beyond, dark
and gloomy, with romance in its depths and
moonshine on its upper banks of snow. The
sky was aglow with stars, and a little flickering
northern light appeared in one quarter of the
horizon, but did not spread. A short distance
from the window, down toward the lake, there
were some trees whose shadows kept prowling
from one to the other, but the great ash stood
alone, writing on the snow.

The night was very still, — only now and
then something shrieked and howled with a
long, wailing cry.

"What is that?" asked Arne.

"It is the weather-vane," said Eli; and afterwards she continued more softly, as though to
herself: "It must have been let loose."

But Arne had been feeling like one who
wanted to speak and could not. Now he said:—

"Do you remember the story about the
thrushes that sang?"

"Yes."

"Why, to be sure, it was you who told that
one! It was a pretty story."

She said, in so gentle a voice that it seemed as though it were the first time he heard it, —

"I often think there is something that sings when it is quite still."

"That is the good within ourselves."

She looked at him as though there were something too much in that answer; they were both quiet afterward. Then she asked, as she traced figures with one finger on the window-pane, —

"Have you made any songs lately?"

He blushed; but this she did not see. Therefore she asked again, —

"How do you manage when you make songs?"

"Would you really like to know?"

"Oh, yes."

"I hoard up the thoughts that others are in the habit of letting go," he answered evasively.

She was long silent, for she had doubtless been making an attempt at a song or two. What if she had had those thoughts and let them go.

"That is strange, said she, as though to herself, and fell to tracing figures on the pane again.

"I made a song after I had seen you the first time."

"Where was that?"

"Over by the parsonage, the evening you left there. I saw you in the lake."

She laughed, then was still a while.

"Let me hear that song."

Arne had never before done such a thing, but now he sang for her the song, —

> "Fair Venevill bounded on lithesome feet,
>   Her lover to meet," etc.

Eli stood there very attentive; she stood there long after he was through. At last she burst out, —

"Oh, how I pity her!"

"It seems as though I had not made it myself," said Arne, for he felt ashamed at having produced it. Nor did he understand how he had come to do so. He remained standing there as if looking after the song.

Then she said: "But I hope it will not be that way with me!"

"No, no, no! I was only thinking of myself."

"Is that to be your fate, then?"

"I do not know; but I felt so at that time —indeed, I do not understand it now, but I once had such a heavy heart."

"That was strange." She began to write on the window-pane again.

The next day, when Arne came in to dinner he went over to the window. Outside it was gray and foggy, within warm and pleasant; but on the window-pane a finger had traced "Arne, Arne, Arne!" and over again "Arne." It was the window where Eli had stood the preceding evening.

But Eli did not come down-stairs that day; she was feeling ill. She had not been well at all of late; she had said so herself, and it was plainly to be seen.

CHAPTER XI.

A DAY later Arne came in and announced that he had just heard on the gard that the priest's daughter Mathilde had that very moment started for the town, as she thought, for a few days, but, as had been decided, to stay there for a year or two. Eli had heard nothing of this before, and fell fainting.

It was the first time Arne had seen any one faint, and he was much alarmed; he ran for the maid-servants, they went for the parents, who started at once; there was confusion all over the gard, even the shepherd-dog barked on the barn-bridge. When Arne came in again, later, the mother was on her knees by the bedside, the father stood holding the sick girl's head. The maid-servants were running, one for water, another for medicine, which was kept in a cupboard, a third was unfastening Eli's jacket at the throat.

"The Lord help and bless us!" cried the mother. "It was certainly wrong that we said nothing to her; it was you, Baard, who would have it so. The Lord help and bless us !"

Baard made no reply.

"I said we had better tell her; but nothing is ever done as I wish. The Lord help and bless us! You are always so underhand with her, Baard; you do not understand her; you do not know what it is to care for any one."

Baard still made no reply.

"She is not like others; they can bear sorrow, but it completely upsets her, poor thing, she is so slight. And especially now when she is not well at all. Wake up again, my dear child, and we will be kind to you! Wake up again, Eli, my own dear child, and do not grieve us so !"

Then Baard said,—

"You are either too silent, or you talk too much;" and he looked over at Arne, as though he did not wish him to hear all this, but to go away. As the maid-servants remained in the room, however, Arne thought that he might stay, too, but he walked to the window. Now the patient rallied so far that she could look about her and recognize people; but at the same moment her memory returned; she shrieked "Mathilde," burst into hysterical weeping, and sobbed until it was painful to be in the

room with her. The mother tried to comfort
her; the father had placed himself where he
might be seen; but the sick girl waved her
hand to them. "Go away!" she cried, "I do
not love you!"

"Good gracious! You do not love your parents?" said the mother.

"No! You are cruel to me, and take from
me the only joy I have!"

"Eli, Eli! Do not speak such dreadful
words!" begged the mother.

"Yes, mother," she shrieked; "now I must
say it! Yes, mother! You want me to marry
that hateful man, and I will not. You shut me
up here, where I am never happy, except when
I am to go out! You take Mathilde from me,
the only person I love and long for in the
world! O God, what will become of me when
Mathilde is no longer here — especially now
that I have so much, so much I cannot manage
when I have no one to talk with?"

"But you really have so seldom been with
her lately," said Baard.

"What did that matter when I had her over
at the window yonder!" answered the sick girl,
and she cried in such a child-like way, that it
seemed to Arne as though he had never before
seen anything like it.

"But you could not see her there," said Baard.

"I could see the gard," answered she; and the mother added, hotly, —

"You do not understand such things at all." Then Baard said no more.

"Now I can never go to the window!" said Eli. "I went there in the morning when I got up; in the evening I sat there in the moonlight: and I went there when I had no one else to go to. Mathilde, Mathilde!"

She writhed in the bed, and again gave way to hysterical weeping. Baard sat down on a stool near by and watched her.

But Eli did not get over this as soon as her parents may have expected. Toward evening they first saw that she was likely to have a protracted illness, the seeds of which had doubtless been gathering for some time; and Arne was called in to assist in carrying her up to her own room. She was unconscious, and lay very pale and still; the mother sat down beside her; the father stood at the foot of the bed and looked on; afterwards he went down to his work. Arne did the same; but that night when he went to bed he prayed for her, prayed that she, young and fair as she was, might have a happy

life, and that no one might shut out joy from
her.

The following day the father and mother sat
talking together when Arne came in; the
mother had been shedding tears. Arne asked
how things were going; each waited for the
other to speak, and therefore it was long before
he got a reply; but finally the father said, "It
looks pretty bad."

Later, Arne heard that Eli had been delir-
ious the whole night; or, as the father said, had
been raving. Now she lay violently ill, knew
no one, would not take any food, and the parents
were just sitting there, deliberating whether
they should call in the doctor. When, later,
they went up-stairs to the sick girl, and Arne
was left alone again, he felt as though life and
death were both up there, but he sat outside.

In a few days, though, she was better. Once
when the father was keeping watch, she took
a fancy to have Narrifas, the bird which Mathilde had given her, standing beside the bed.
Then Baard told her the truth, that in all this
confusion the bird had been forgotten, and that
it was dead. The mother came just while Baard
was telling this, and she burst out in the
door, — "Good gracious me! how heedless you
are, Baard, to tell such things to that sick

child! See, now she is fainting away again; Heaven forgive you for what you have done!"

Every time the patient revived she screamed for the bird, said that it would never go well with Mathilde since Narrifas was dead, wanted to go to her, and fell into a swoon again. Baard stood there and looked on until he could bear it no longer; then he wanted to help wait on her too; but the mother pushed him away, saying that she would take care of the sick girl alone. Then Baard gazed at both of them a long while, after which he put on his cap with both hands, turned, and went out.

The priest and his wife came over later; for the illness had taken fresh hold on Eli, and had become so bad that they knew not whether it was tending to life or death.

Both the priest and the priest's wife reasoned with Baard, and urged that he was too harsh with Eli; they had heard about the bird, and the priest told him bluntly that such conduct was rough; he would take the child home to the parsonage, he said, as soon as she had improved enough to be moved. The priest's wife finally would not even see Baard; she wept and sat with the sick girl, sent for the doctor, took his orders herself, and came over several times each day to carry them out.

Baard went wandering about from place to place in the yard, going chiefly where he could be alone; he would often stand still for a long time, then straighten his cap with both hands, and find something to do.

The mother did not speak to him any more; they scarcely looked at each other. Baard went up to the sick girl's room several times each day; he took off his shoes at the bottom of the stairs, laid down his hat outside of the door, which he opened cautiously. The moment he came in, Birgit would turn as though she had not seen him, and then sit as before, with her head in her hand, looking straight before her and at the sick girl. The latter lay still and pale, unconscious of anything about her. Baard would stand a while at the foot of the bed, look at them both, and say nothing. Once, when Eli moved as though about to awaken, he stole away directly as softly as he had come.

Arne often thought that words had now been exchanged between husband and wife and parents and child, which had been long brewing, and which would not soon be forgotten. He longed to get away, although he would have liked first to know how Eli's illness would end. But this he could learn even if he left, he thought; he went, therefore, to Baard, and said

that he wished to go home; the work for which
he had come was done. Baard sat outside on
the chopping-block when Arne came to tell him
this. He sat digging in the snow with a pin.
Arne knew the pin; for it was the same that
had fastened the weather vane. Without looking up Baard said, —

"I suppose it is not pleasant to be here now,
but I feel as if I did not want you to leave."

Baard said no more; nor did Arne speak.
He stood a while, then went away and busied
himself with some work, as though it were decided that he should remain.

Later, when Arne was called in to dinner,
Baard still sat on the chopping-block. Arne
went over to him and asked how Eli was getting on.

"I think she must be pretty bad to-day,"
said Baard; "I see that mother is crying."

Arne felt as though some one had bidden
him to sit down, and he sat down directly opposite Baard on the end of a fallen tree.

"I have been thinking of your father these
days," said Baard, so unexpectedly, that Arne
could make no reply. "You know, I dare say,
what there was between us two?"

"Yes, I know."

"Ah, well, you only know half, as might

have been expected, and naturally lay the greatest blame on me."

Arne answered presently : " You have doubtless settled that matter with your God, as my
father has surely done."

"Ah, well, that may be as one takes it," answered Baard. "When I found this pin again,
it seemed so strange to me that you should
come here and loosen the vane. Just as well
first as last, thought I." He had taken off his
cap and sat looking into it.

Arne did not yet understand that by this
Baard meant that he now wanted to talk with
him about his father. Indeed, he still did not
understand it, even after Baard was well under
way, so little was this like the man. But what
had been working before in his mind, he gradually comprehended as the story advanced, and
if he had hitherto had respect for this blunder-
ing but thoroughly good man, it was not les-
sened now.

"I might have been about fourteen years
old," said Baard, then paused, as he did from
time to time throughout his whole story, said
a few words more, and paused again in such a
manner that his story bore the strong impress
of having every word weighed. "I might have
been about fourteen years old when I became

acquainted with your father, who was of the same age. He was very wild, and could not bear to have any one above him. And what he never could forgive me was, that I was the head of the class when we were confirmed, and he was number two. He often offered to wrestle with me, but nothing ever came of it; I suppose because we were neither of us sure of ourselves. But it is strange that he fought every day, and no misfortune befell him; the one time I tried my hand it turned out as badly as could be; but, to be sure, I had waited a long time too.

" Nils fluttered about all the girls and they about him. There was only one I wanted, but he took her from me at every dance, at every wedding, at every party; it was the one to whom I am now married. . . . I often had a desire, as I sat looking on, to make a trial of strength with him, just because of this matter; but I was afraid I might lose, and I knew that if I did so I should lose her too. When the others had gone, I would lift the weights he had lifted, kick the beam he had kicked, but the next time he danced away from me with the girl, I did not dare tackle him, although it chanced once, as Nils stood joking with her right before my face, that I laid hold of a good sized fellow who stood by and tossed him against

the beam, as though for sport. Nils grew pale,
too, that time.

" If he had only been kind to the girl; but
he was false to her, and that evening after evening. I almost think she cared more for him
each time. Then it was that the last thing
happened. I thought now it must either break
or bear. Nor did the Lord want him to go
about any longer; and therefore he fell a little
more heavily than I had intended. I never saw
him after that."

They sat for a long time silent. Finally
Baard continued : —

" I offered myself again. She answered
neither yes nor no; and so I thought she
would like me better afterwards. We were
married; the wedding took place down in the
valley, at the house of her father's sister, who
left her property to her; we began with plenty,
and what we then had has increased. Our
gards lay alongside of each other, and they have
since been thrown into one, as had been my idea
from boyhood up. But many other things did
not turn out as I had planned."

He was long silent; Arne thought, for a
while, he was weeping; it was not so. But he
spoke in a still gentler tone than usual when he
began again, —

" At first she was quiet and very sorrowful. I had nothing to say for her comfort, and so I was silent. Later, she fell at times into that commanding way that you have perhaps noticed in her; yet it was after all a change, and so I was silent then, too. But a truly happy day I have not had since I was married, and that has been now for twenty years."

He broke the pin in two; then he sat a while looking at the pieces.

" When Eli grew to be a large girl, I thought she would find more happiness among strangers than here. It is seldom that I have insisted on anything; it usually has been wrong, too, when I have; and so it was with this. The mother yearned for her child, although only the lake parted them; and at last I found out that Eli was not under the best influences over at the parsonage, for there is really much good-natured nonsense about the priest's family; but I found it out too late. Now she seems to care for neither father nor mother."

He had taken his cap off again; now his long hair fell over his eyes; he stroked it aside, and put on his cap with both hands, as though about to go; but as in getting up he turned toward the house, he stopped and added, with a glance at the chamber window, —

"I thought it was best she and Mathilde should not bid each other good-by; but that proved to be wrong. I told her the little bird was dead, for it was my fault, you know, and it seemed to me right to confess; but that was wrong too. And so it is with everything. I have always meant to do the best, but it has turned out to be the worst; and now it has gone so far that they speak ill of me, both wife and daughter, and I am alone here."

A girl now called out to them that dinner was getting cold. Baard got up. "I hear the horses neighing," said he, "somebody must have forgotten them;" and with this he went over to the stable to give them hay.

CHAPTER XII.

ELI was very weak after her illness; the mother sat over her night and day, and was never down-stairs; the father made his usual visits up to the sick-room in his stocking feet, and leaving his cap outside of the door. Arne was still at the gard; he and the father sat together of evenings; he had come to think a good deal of Baard, who was a well-educated man, a deep thinker, but seemed to be afraid of what he knew. Arne helped him to get things right in his mind and told him much that he did not know before, and Baard was very grateful.

Eli could now sit up at intervals; and as she began to improve she took many fancies into her head. Thus it was that one evening as Arne sat in the room below Eli's chamber singing songs in a loud voice, the mother came down and brought word that Eli wanted to know if he would not come up-stairs and sing that she might hear the words. Arne had undoubtedly been singing for Eli all along; for when her

mother gave him the message he grew red, and
rose as though he would deny what he had been
doing, although no one had charged him with
it. He soon recovered his composure, and said
evasively that there was very little he could
sing. But the mother remarked that it did not
seem so when he was alone.

Arne yielded and went. He had not seen
Eli since the day he had helped carry her up-
stairs; he felt that she must now be greatly
changed, and was almost afraid to see her. But
when he softly opened the door and entered, it
was so dark in the room that he saw no one.
He paused on the threshold.

"Who is it?" asked Eli, in a clear, low
voice.

"It is Arne Kampen," he answered, in a
guarded tone, that the words might fall softly.

"It was kind of you to come."

"How are you now, Eli?"

"Thank you, I am better."

"Please sit down, Arne," said she, presently, and Arne felt his way to a chair that
stood by the foot of the bed. "It was so nice
to hear you singing, you must sing a little for
me up here."

"If I only knew anything that was suitable."

There was silence for a moment: then she

said, " Sing a hymn," and he did so ; it was a
part of one of the confirmation hymns. When
he had finished, he heard that she was weeping,
and so he dared not sing any more ; but presently she said, " Sing another one like that,"
and he sang another, choosing the one usually
sung when the candidates for confirmation are
standing in the church aisle.

" How many things I have thought of while
I have been lying here," said Eli. He did not
know what to answer, and he heard her weeping quietly in the dark. A clock was ticking
on the wall, it gave warning that it was about
to strike, and then struck; Eli drew a long
breath several times as though she would ease
her breast, and then she said, " One knows so
little. I have known neither father nor mother.
I have not been kind to them, — and that is
why it gives me such strange feelings to hear
that confirmation hymn."

When people talk in the dark, they are always more truthful than when they see each
other face to face ; they can say more, too.

" It is good to hear your words," replied
Arne ; he was thinking of what she had said
when she was taken ill.

She knew what he meant ; and so she remarked, " Had not this happened to me, God

only knows how long it might have been before
I had found my mother."

"She has been talking with you now?"

"Every day; she has done nothing else."

"Then, I dare say, you have heard many
things."

"You may well say so."

"I suppose she talked about my father?"

"Yes."

"Does she still think of him?"

"She does."

"He was not kind to her."

"Poor mother!"

"He was worst of all, though, to himself."
Thoughts now arose that neither liked to
express to the other. Eli was the first to break
the silence.

"They say you are like your father."

"So I have heard," he answered, evasively.

She paid no heed to the tone of his voice;
and so, after a while, she continued, "Could he,
too, make songs?"

"No."

"Sing a song for me,—one you have made
yourself."

But Arne was not in the habit of confessing
that the songs he sang were his own. "I have
none," said he.

"Indeed you have, and I am sure you will sing them for me if I ask it."

What he had never done for others, he now did for her.   He sang the following song: —

" The tree's early leaf-buds were bursting their brown:
    ' Shall I take them away?' said the frost, sweeping down.
        'No, dear; leave them alone
        Till blossoms here have grown,'
    Prayed the tree, while it trembled from rootlet to crown.

" The tree bore its blossoms, and all the birds sung:
    ' Shall I take them away?' said the wind, as it swung.
        ' No, dear; leave them alone
        Till berries here have grown,'
    Said the tree, while its leaflets all quivering hung.

" The tree bore its fruit in the midsummer glow:
    Said the girl, ' May I gather thy berries or no?'
        ' Yes, dear, all thou canst see;
        Take them; all are for thee,'
    Said the tree, while it bent down its laden boughs low." [1]

This song almost took her breath away.   He, too, sat there silent, after he was through, as though he had sung more than he cared to say to her.

Darkness has great power over those who are sitting in it and dare not speak; they are never so near each other as then.   If Eli only turned, only moved her hand on the bed-cover, only breathed a little more heavily than usual, Arne heard it.

[1] Adapted to the metre of the original from the translation of Augusta Plesner and S. Rugeley-Powers.

"Arne, could not you teach me to make songs?"

"Have you never tried?"

"Yes, these last few days I have; but I have not succeeded."

"Why, what did you want to have in them?"

"Something about my mother, who cared so much for your father."

"That is a sad theme."

"I have cried over it, too."

"You must not think of what you are going to put in your songs; it comes of itself."

"How does it come?"

"As other precious things, when you least expect it."

They were both silent.

"I wonder, Arne, that you are longing to go away when you have so much that is beautiful within yourself."

"Do *you* know that I am longing?"

She made no reply to this, but lay still a few moments, as though in thought.

"Arne, you must not go away!" said she, and this sent a glow through him.

"Well, sometimes I have less desire to go."

"Your mother must be very fond of you. I should like to see your mother."

"Come over to Kampen when you are well."

And now all at once he pictured her sitting in the cheerful room at Kampen, looking out on the mountains; his chest began to heave, the blood rushed to his head. "It is warm in here," said he, getting up.

She heard this. "Are you going, Arne?" asked she, and he sat down again.

"You must come over to us often; mother likes you so much."

"I should be glad to come myself; but I must have some errand, though."

Eli was silent for a while, as if she were considering something. "I believe," said she, "that mother has something she wants to ask of you."

He heard her turn in bed. There was no sound to be heard, either in the room or outside, save the ticking of the clock on the wall. At last she burst out,—

"How I wish it were summer!"

"That it were summer?" and there rose up in his mind, blended with fragrant foliage and the tinkling of cattle bells, shouts from the mountains, singing from the valleys, Black Water glittering in the sunshine, the gards rocking in it, and Eli coming out and sitting down, as she had done that evening long ago.

10

"If it were summer," said she, "and I were sitting on the hill, I really believe I could sing a song."

He laughed and asked: "What would it be about?"

"Oh, something easy, about — I do not know myself — "

"Tell me, Eli!" and he sprang up in delight; then, recollecting himself, he sat down again.

"No; not for all the world!" She laughed.

"I sang for you when you asked me."

"Yes, you did; but — no! no!"

"Eli, do you think I would make sport of your little verse?"

"No; I do not think so, Arne; but it is not anything I have made myself."

"It is by some one else, then."

"Yes, it just came floating of itself."

"Then you can surely repeat it to me."

"No, no; it is not altogether that either, Arne. Do not ask me any more." She must have hid her face in the bedclothes, for the last words seemed to come out of them.

"You are not as kind to me now, Eli, as I was to you!" he said, and rose.

"Arne, there is a difference — you do not understand me — but it was — I do not know myself — another time — do not be angry with me, Arne! Do not go away from me!" She began to weep.

"Eli, what is the matter?" He listened. "Are you feeling ill?" He did not think she was. She still wept; he thought that he must either go forward or backward.

"Eli!"

"Yes!"

They both spoke in whispers.

"Give me your hand!"

She did not answer; he listened intently, eagerly, felt about on the coverlid, and clasped a warm little hand that lay outside.

They heard steps on the stairs, and let go of each other's hands. It was Eli's mother, who was bringing in a light. "You are sitting quite too long in the dark," said she, and put the candlestick on the table. But neither Eli nor Arne could bear the light; she turned toward the pillow, he held his hand up before his eyes. "Oh, yes; it hurts the eyes a little at first," said her mother; "but that will soon pass off."

Arne searched on the floor for the cap he did not have with him, and then he left the room.

The next day he heard that Eli was coming
down-stairs for a little while after dinner.   He
gathered together his tools, and said good-by.
When she came down he was gone.

CHAPTER XIII.

SPRING comes late in the mountains. The mail that passed along the highway during the winter three times a week, in April only passes once, and the inhabitants know then that in the outside world the snow is thawed, the ice broken; that the steamers are running, and the plow put into the earth. Here, the snow still lies three ells deep; the cattle low in the stalls, and the birds come, but hide themselves, shivering with the cold. Occasionally some traveler arrives, saying he has left his cart down in the valley, and he has flowers with him, which he shows,—he has gathered them by the wayside. Then the people become restless, go about talking together, look at the sky and down in the valley, wondering how much the sun gains each day. They strew ashes on the snow, and think of those who are now gathering flowers.

It was at such a time that old Margit Kampen came walking up to the parsonage and asked to speak with "father."[1] She was invited into

---

[1] The peasants call the priest father.

the study, where the priest, a slender, fair-haired, gentle-looking man with large eyes and spectacles, received her kindly, knew who she was, and asked her to sit down.

" Is it now something about Arne again? " he inquired, as though they had often talked together about him.

" Heaven help me ! " said Margit ; " it is never anything but good I have to say of him, and yet my heart is so heavy. She looked very sad as she spoke.

" Has that longing come back again ? " asked the priest.

" Worse than ever," said the mother. " I do not even believe he will stay with me until spring comes to us here."

"And yet he has promised never to leave you."

" True enough ; but, dear me, he must manage for himself now ; when the mind is set upon going, go one must, I suppose. But what will become of me ? "

" Still I will believe, as long as possible, that he will not leave you," said the priest.

" Certainly not ; but what if he should never be content at home? I would then have it on my conscience that I stood in his way. There are times when I think I ought to ask him myself to go away."

"How do you know that he is longing now more than ever?"

"Oh, from many things. Since midwinter he has not worked out in the parish a single day. On the other hand, he has made three trips to town, and has stayed away a long while each time. He scarcely ever talks now when he is working, as he often used to do. He sits for hours by the little window up-stairs, and looks out over the mountains in the direction of the Kamp gorge; he sometimes stays there a whole Sunday afternoon, and often when it is moonlight, he sits there far into the night."

"Does he never read to you?"

"Of course he reads and sings to me every Sunday; but he always seems in a hurry, except now and then, when he overdoes it."

"Does he never come and talk with you?"

"He often lets so long a time pass without saying a word, that I cannot help crying when I sit alone. Then, I suppose, he sees this, for he begins to talk with me, but it is always about trifles, never about anything serious."

The priest was walking up and down; now he stopped and asked, "Why do you not speak with him about it?"

It was some time before she made any reply to this; she sighed several times, she looked

first downward, then on either side, — she folded
the handkerchief she carried.

"I came here to-day to have a talk with father about something that lies heavily on my
heart."

"Speak freely, it will lighten the burden."

"I know that; for I have now dragged it
along alone these many years, and it grows
heavier each year."

"What is it, my good woman?"

There was a brief pause; then she said, "I
have sinned greatly against my son," — and she
began to cry.

The priest came close up to her. "Confess
it to me," said he, "then we will together pray
God that you may be forgiven."

Margit sobbed and dried her eyes, but began
to weep afresh as soon as she tried to speak,
and this was repeated several times. The
priest comforted her, and said she surely could
not have been guilty of anything very sinful,
that she was no doubt too strict with herself,
and so on. Margit wept, however, and could
not muster the courage to begin until the priest
had seated himself by her side and spoken
kindly words to her. Then, in broken sentences, she faltered forth her confession: —

"He had a hard time of it when he was a

boy, and so his mind became bent on travel.
Then he met Kristian, he who has grown so
very rich over there where they dig for gold.
Kristian gave Arne so many books that he
ceased to be like the rest of us; they sat together in the long evenings, and when Kristian
went away, my boy longed to follow him. Just
at that time, though, his father fell down dead,
and Arne promised never to leave me. Yet I
was like a hen that had brooded a duck's egg,
when the young duckling had burst the shell,
he wanted to go out on the great water, and I
remained on the bank screaming. If he did
not actually go away himself, his heart went in
his songs, and every morning I thought I would
find his bed empty.

" Then there came a letter for him from a
far-off country, and I knew it must be from
Kristian. God forgive me, I hid it! I thought
that would be the end of the matter, but still
another one came, and as I had kept the first
from him, I had to keep the second one too
But, indeed, it seemed as though they would
burn a hole in the chest where they lay, for
my thoughts would go there from the time I
opened my eyes in the morning until I closed
them at night. And you never have known
anything so bad as this, for there came a third!

I stood holding it in my hand for a quarter of
an hour; I carried it in my bosom for three
days, weighing within me whether I should
give it to him or lay it away with the others,
but perhaps it would have power to lure the
boy away from me, and I could not help it, I
put the letter away with the others. Now I
went about in sorrow every day, both because
of those that were in the chest and because of
the new ones that might come. I was afraid
of every person who came to our house. When
we were in the house together, and there came
a knock at the door, I trembled, for it might be
a letter, and then *he* would get it. When he
was out in the parish, I kept thinking at home
that now perhaps he would get a letter while
he was away, and that it might have something
in it about those that had come before. When
he was coming home, I watched his face in the
distance, and, dear me! how happy I was when
I saw him smiling, for then I knew he had no
letter! He had grown so handsome, too, just
like his father, but much fairer and more gentle-looking. And then he had such a voice for
singing: when he sat outside of the door at
sunset, singing toward the mountain ridge and
listening for the echo, I felt in my heart that I
never could live without him! If I only saw

him, or if I knew he was anywhere around, and he looked tolerably happy, and would only give me a word now and then, I wished for nothing more on earth, and would not have had a single tear unshed.

"But just as he seemed to be getting on better, and to be feeling more at ease among people, there came word from the parish post-office that a fourth letter had now come, and that in it there were two hundred dollars! I thought I should drop right down on the spot where I stood. What should I do now? The letter, of course, I could get out of the way; but the money? I could not sleep for several nights on account of this money. I kept it up in the garret for a while, then left it in the cellar behind a barrel, and once I was so beside myself that I laid it in the window so that he might find it. When I heard him coming, I took it away again. At last I found a way, though I gave him the money and said it had been out at interest since mother's lifetime. He spent it in improving the gard, as had been in my own mind, and there it was not lost. But then it happened that same autumn that he sat one evening wondering why Kristian had so entirely forgotten him.

"Now the wound opened afresh, and the

money burned. What I had done was a sin, and the sin had been of no use to me !

"The mother who has sinned against her own child is the most unhappy of all mothers, — and yet I only did it out of love. So I shall be punished, I dare say, by losing what is dearest to me. For since midwinter he has taken up again the tune he sings when he is longing ; he has sung it from boyhood up, and I never hear it without growing pale. Then I feel I could give up all for him, and now you shall see for yourself," — she took a scrap of paper out of her bosom, unfolded it, and gave it to the priest, — "here is something he is writing at from time to time ; it certainly belongs to that song. I brought it with me, for I cannot read such fine writing ; please see if there is anything in it about his going away."

There was only one stanza on this paper. For the second one there were half and whole lines here and there, as if it were a song he had forgotten, and was now calling to mind again, verse by verse. The first stanza ran, —

> "Oh, how I wonder what I should see
>   Over the lofty mountains !
> Snow here shuts out the view from me,
> Round about stands the green pine-tree,
>   Longing to hasten over —
>   Dare it become a rover?

"Is it about his going away?" asked Margit, her eyes fixed eagerly on the priest's face.

"Yes, it is," answered he, and let the paper drop.

"Was I not sure of it! Ah, me! I know that tune so well!" She looked at the priest, her hands folded, anxious, intent, while tear after tear trickled down her cheek.

But the priest knew as little how to advise as she. "The boy must be left to himself in this matter," said he. "Life cannot be altered for his sake, but it depends on himself whether he shall one day find out its meaning. Now it seems he wants to go away to do so."

"But was it not just so with the old woman?" said Margit.

"With the old woman?" repeated the priest.

"Yes; she who went out to fetch the sunshine into her house, instead of cutting windows in the walls."

The priest was astonished at her shrewdness; but it was not the first time she had surprised him when she was on this theme; for Margit, indeed, had not thought of anything else for seven or eight years.

"Do you think he will leave me? What shall I do? And the money? And the letters?" All this crowded upon her at once.

"Well, it was not right about the letters.
You can hardly be justified in withholding
from your son what belonged to him. It was
still worse, however, to place a fellow Chris-
tian in a bad light when it was not deserved,
and the worst of all was that it was one whom
Arne loved and who was very fond of him in
return. But we will pray God to forgive you,
we will both pray."

Margit bowed her head; she still sat with
her hands folded.

"How earnestly I would pray him for forgiveness, if I only knew he would stay!" She
was probably confounding in her mind the
Lord and Arne.

The priest pretended he had not noticed
this. "Do you mean to confess this to him at
once?" he asked.

She looked down and said in a low tone,
"If I dared wait a little while I should like to
do so."

The priest turned aside to hide a smile, as he
asked, "Do you not think your sin becomes
greater the longer you delay the confession?"

Both hands were busied with her handkerchief: she folded it into a very small square,
and tried to get it into a still smaller one, but
that was not possible.

"If I confess about the letters, I am afraid he will leave me."

"You dare not place your reliance on the Lord, then?"

"Why, to be sure I do!" she said hurriedly; then she added softly, "But what if he should go anyway?"

"So, then, you are more afraid of Arne's leaving you than of continuing in sin?"

Margit had unfolded her handkerchief again; she put it now to her eyes, for she was beginning to weep.

The priest watched her for a while, then he continued: "Why did you tell me all this when you did not mean it to lead to anything?" He waited a long time, but she did not answer. "You thought, perhaps, your sin would become less when you had confessed it?"

"I thought that it would," said she, softly, with her head bowed still farther down on her breast.

The priest smiled and got up. "Well, well, my dear Margit, you must act so that you will have joy in your old age."

"If I could only keep what I have!" said she; and the priest thought she dared not imagine any greater happiness than living in her constant state of anxiety. He smiled as he lit his pipe.

"If we only had a little girl who could get hold of him, then you should see that he would stay!"

She looked up quickly, and her eyes followed the priest until he paused in front of her.

" Eli Böen? What " —

She colored and looked down again; but she made no reply.

The priest, who had stood still, waiting, said finally, but this time in quite a low tone "What if we should arrange it so that they should meet oftener at the parsonage?"

She glanced up at the priest to find out whether he was really in earnest. But she did not quite dare believe him.

The priest had begun to walk up and down again, but now he paused. "See here, Margit! When it comes to the point, perhaps this was your whole errand here to-day, hey?"

She bowed her head far down, she thrust two fingers into the folded handkerchief, and brought out a corner of it. "Well, yes, God help me; that was exactly what I wanted."

The priest burst out laughing, and rubbed his hands. "Perhaps that was what you wanted the last time you were here, too?"

She drew the corner of the handkerchief farther out; she stretched it and stretched it. "Since you ask me, yes, it was just that."

"Ha, ha, ha, ha! Ah, Margit! Margit! We shall see what we can do; for, to tell the truth, my wife and daughter have for a long time had the same thoughts as you."

"Is it possible?" She looked up, at once so happy and so bashful, that the priest had his own delight in her open, pretty face, in which the childlike expression had been preserved through all sorrow and anxiety.

"Ah, well, Margit, you, whose love is so great, will, I have no doubt, obtain forgiveness, for love's sake, both from your God and from your son, for the wrong you have done. You have probably been punished enough already in the continual, wearing anxiety you have lived in; we shall, if God is willing, bring this to a speedy end, for, if He *wishes* this, He will help us a little now."

She drew a long sigh, which she repeated again and again; then she arose, gave her thanks, dropped a courtesy, and courtesied again at the door. But she was scarcely well outside before a change came over her. She cast upward a look beaming with gratitude, and she hurried more and more the farther she

11

got away from people, and lightly as she tripped
down toward Kampen that day, she had not
done for many, many years. When she got
so far on her way that she could see the thick
smoke curling gayly up from the chimney, she
blessed the house, the whole gard, the priest,
and Arne, — and then remembered that they
were going to have smoked beef for dinner, —
her favorite dish !

CHAPTER XIV.

KAMPEN was a beautiful gard. It lay in the midst of a plain, bordered below by the Kamp gorge, and above by the parish road; on the opposite side of the road was a thick wood, a little farther beyond, a rising mountain ridge, and behind this the blue, snow-capped mountains. On the other side of the gorge there was also a broad mountain range, which first entirely surrounded Black Water on the side where Böen lay, then grew higher toward Kampen, but at the same time turned aside to make way for the broad basin called the lower parish, and which began just below, for Kampen was the last gard in the upper parish.

The front door of the dwelling-house was turned toward the road; it was probably about two thousand paces off; a path with leafy birch-trees on either side led thither. The wood lay on both sides of the clearing; the fields and meadows could, therefore, extend as far as the owners themselves wished; it was in all respects a most excellent gard. A little garden

lay in front of the house. Arne managed it as
his books directed. To the left were the sta-
bles and other out-houses. They were nearly
all new built, and formed a square opposite the
dwelling-house. The latter was painted red,
with white window-frames and doors, was two
stories high, thatched with turf, and small
shrubs grew on the roof; the one gable had a
vane staff, on which turned an iron cock, with
high, spread tail.

Spring had come to the mountain districts.
It was a Sunday morning; there was a little
heaviness in the air, but it was calm and without frost; mist hung over the wood, but Margit thought it would lift during the day. Arne
had read the sermon for his mother and sung
the hymns, which had done him good; now he
was in full trim, ready to go up to the parsonage. He opened the door, the fresh perfume of
the leaves was wafted toward him, the garden
lay dew-covered and bowed by the morning
mist, and from the Kamp gorge there came
a roaring, mingled at intervals with mighty
booms, making everything tremble to the ear
and the eye.

Arne walked upward. The farther he got
from the force the less awe-inspiring became its
roar, which finally spread itself like the deep
tones of an organ over the whole landscape.

" The Lord be with him on his way ! " said
the mother, opening the window and looking
after him until the shrubbery closed about him.
The fog lifted more and more, the sun cut
through it ; there was life now about the fields
and in the garden ; all Arne's work sprouted
out in fresh growth, sending fragrance and joy
up to the mother. Spring is lovely to those
who long have been surrounded by winter.

Arne had no fixed errand at the parsonage,
but still he wanted to learn about the papers
he and the priest took together. Recently he
had seen the names of several Norsemen who
had done remarkably well digging gold in
America, and among them was Kristian. Now
Arne had heard a rumor that Kristian was expected home. He could, no doubt, get infor-
mation about this at the parsonage, — and if
Kristian had really returned, then Arne would
go to him in the interval between spring and
haying time. This was working in his mind
until he had advanced so far that he could see
Black Water, and Böen on the other side. The
fog had lifted there, too ; the sun was playing
on the green, the mountain loomed up with
shining peak, but the fog was still lying in its
lap ; the wood darkened the water on the right
side, but in front of the house the ground was

more flat, and its white sand glittered in the
sunshine. Suddenly his thoughts sped to the
red-painted building with white doors and window-frames, that he had had in mind when he
painted his own. He did not remember those
first gloomy days he had passed there; he only
thought of that bright summer they had both
seen, he and Eli, up beside her sick-bed. Since
then he had not been to Böen, nor would he go
there, not for the whole world. If only his
thoughts barely touched on it, he grew crimson
and abashed; and yet this happened again
every day, and many times a day. If there
was anything which could drive him out of the
parish, it was just this!

Onward he went, as though he would flee
from his thoughts, but the farther he walked
the nearer opposite Böen he came, and the more
he gazed upon it. The fog was entirely gone,
the sky clear from one mountain outline to the
other, the birds sailed along and called aloud to
one another in the glad sunny air, the fields re-
sponded with millions of flowers; the Kamp
force did not here compel gladness to bow the
knee in submission and awe, but buoyant and
frolicsome it tumbled over, singing, twinkling,
rejoicing without end!

Arne had walked till he was in a glowing

heat ; he flung himself down in the grass at the
foot of a hill, looked over towards Böen, then
turned away to avoid seeing it.   Presently he
heard singing above him, pure and clear, as song
had never sounded to him before ; it floated out
over the meadow, mingled with the chattering
of the birds, and he was scarcely sure of the
tune before he recognized the words too, — for
the tune was his favorite one, and the words
were those that had been working in his mind
from the time he was a boy, and forgotten the
same day he had brought them forth !   He
sprang up as though he would catch them, then
paused and listened ; here came the first stanza,
here came the second, here came the third and
the fourth of his own forgotten song stream
ing down to him : —

> " Oh, how I wonder what I should see
>   Over the lofty mountains !
> Snow here shuts out the view from me,
> Round about stands the green pine-tree,
>   Longing to hasten over —
>   Dare it become a rover ?

> " Soars the eagle with strong wing play,
>   Over the lofty mountains ;
> Rows through the young and vigorous day
> Sating his courage in quest of prey ;
>   When he will swooping downward,
>   Tow'rd far-off lands gazing onward.

"Leaf-heavy apple, wilt thou net go
       Over the lofty mountains?
Forth putting buds 'mid summer's glow,
Thou wilt till next time wait, I know;
          All of these birds art swinging,
          Knowing not what they 're singing.

"He who for twenty years longed to flee
       Over the lofty mountains,
Nor beyond them can hope to see,
Smaller each year feels himself to be;
          Hears what the birds are singing,
          Thou art with confidence swinging.

"Bird, with thy chatt'ring, what wouldst thou here
       Over the lofty mountains?
Fairer the lands beyond must appear,
Higher the trees and the skies far more clear.
          Wouldst thou but longing be bringing,
          Bird, but no wings with thy singing?

"Shall I the journey never take
       Over the lofty mountains?
Must my poor thoughts on this rock-wall break?
Must it a dread, ice-bound prison make,
          Shutting at last in around me,
          Till for my tomb it surround me?

"Forth will I! forth! Oh, far, far away,
       Over the lofty mountains!
I will be crushed and consumed if I stay;
Courage tow'rs up and seeks the way,
          Let it its flight now be taking,
          Not on this rock-wall be breaking!

"One day I know I shall wander afar
       Over the lofty mountains!
Lord, my God, is thy door ajar?

Good is thy home where the blessed are;
Keep it though closed a while longer,
Till my deep longing grow stronger." [1]

Arne stood still until the last verse, the last
word, had died away. Again he heard the birds
sporting and twittering, but he knew not
whether he himself dared stir. Find out who
had been singing, though, he must; he raised
his foot and trod so carefully that he could
not hear the grass rustle. A little butterfly
alighted on a flower, directly at his feet, had
to start up again, flew only a little piece farther, had to start up again, and so on all over
the hill as he crept cautiously up. Soon he
came to a leafy bush, and cared to go no farther, for now he could see. A bird flew up
from the bush, gave a startled cry and darted
over the sloping hill-side, and then she who
was sitting within view looked up. Arne
stooped far down, holding his breath, his heart
throbbing so wildly that he heard its every
beat, listening, not daring to move a leaf, for
it was, indeed, she, — it was Eli whom he
saw!

After a long, long while, he looked up just
a little, and would gladly have drawn a step
nearer; but he thought the bird might per-

[1] Auber Forestier's translation.

haps have its nest under the bush, and was afraid he would tread on it. He peered out between the leaves as they blew aside and closed together again. The sun shone directly on her. She wore a black dress without sleeves,[1] and had a boy's straw hat perched lightly on her head, and slanting a little to one side. In her lap lay a book, and on it a profusion of wild flowers; her right hand was dreamily toying with them; in her left, which rested on her knee, her head was bowed. She was gazing in the direction of the bird's flight, and it really seemed as though she had been weeping.

Anything more lovely Arne had neither seen nor dreamed of in his whole life; the sun, too, had scattered all its gold over her and the spot where she was sitting, and the song still floated about her, although its last notes had long since been sung, so that he thought, breathed — aye, even his heart beat in time to it.

She took up the book and opened it, but soon closed it again and sat as before, beginning to hum something else. It was, "The tree's early leaf-buds were bursting their brown." He knew it at once, although she did not quite remember either the words or the tune, and

---

[1] Peasants wear an under-garment high in the neck with long sleeves.

made many mistakes. The stanza she knew best was the last one, therefore she often repeated it; but she sang it thus: —

" The tree bore its berries, so mellow and red:
' May I gather thy berries ? ' a sweet maiden said.
'Yes, dear; all thou canst see;
    Take them; all are for thee; '
Said the tree — trala-lala, trala, lala — said." [1]

Then suddenly she sprang up, scattering the flowers all around her, and sang aloud, so that the tune, as it quivered through the air, could easily be heard all the way over to Böen. And then she ran away. Should he call after her? No! There she went skipping over the hills, singing, trolling; her hat fell off, she picked it up again; and then she stood still in the midst of the tallest grass.

"Shall I call after her? She is looking round ! "

He quickly stooped down. It was a long while before he dared peep forth again; at first he only raised his head; he could not see her: then he drew himself up on his knees, and still could not see her; finally, he got all the way up. No, she was gone !

He no longer wanted to go to the parsonage. He wanted nothing !

[1] Adapted to the original metre from the translation of Augusta Plesner and S. Rugeley-Powers.

Later he sat where she had been sitting, still sat there until the sun drew near the meridian. The lake was not ruffled by a single ripple; the smoke from the gards began to curl upward; the land-rails, one after another, had ceased their call; the small birds, though, continued their sportive gambols, but withdrew to the wood; the dew was gone and the grass looked sober; not a breath of wind stirred the leaves; it was about an hour from noon. Arne scarcely knew how it was that he found himself seated there, weaving together a little song; a sweet melody offered itself for it, and into a heart curiously full of all that was gentle, the tune came and went until the picture was complete. He sang the song calmly as he had made it : —

" He went in the forest the whole day long,
        The whole day long;
    For there he had heard such a wonderful song,
        A wonderful song.

" He fashioned a flute from a willow spray,
        A willow spray,
    To see if within it the sweet tune lay,
        The sweet tune lay.

" It whispered and told him its name at last,
        Its name at last;
    But then, while he listened, away it passed,
        Away it passed.

" But oft when he slumbered, again it stole,
        Again it stole,

With touches of love upon his soul,
    Upon his soul.

" Then he tried to catch it, and keep it fast,
    And keep it fast ;
But he woke, and away in the night it passed,
    In the night it passed.

" ' My Lord, let me pass in the night, I pray,
    In the night, I pray ;
For the tune has taken my heart away,
    My heart away.'

" Then answered the Lord, ' It is thy friend,
    It is thy friend,
Though not for an hour shall thy longing end,
    Thy longing end ;

" ' And all the others are nothing to thee,
    Nothing to thee,
To this that thou seekest and never shalt see,
    Never shalt see.' " [1]

[1] Translated by Augusta Plesner and S. Rugeley-Powers.

CHAPTER XV.

IT was a Sunday evening in midsummer
the priest had returned from church, and Margit had been sitting with him until it was nearly
seven o'clock. Now she took her leave, and
hastened down the steps and out into the yard,
for there she had just caught sight of Eli Böen,
who had been playing for some time with the
priest's son and her own brother.

" Good evening ! " said Margit, standing still,
" and God bless you all ! "

" Good evening ! " replied Eli, blushing crimson, and showing a desire to stop playing, although the boys urged her to continue ; but
she begged to be excused, and they had to let
her go for that evening.

"It seems to me I ought to know you," said
Margit.

" That is quite likely," was the reply.

' This surely never can be Eli Böen ? "

Yes, it was she.

" Oh, dear me ! So you are Eli Böen ! Yes,
now I see you are like your mother."

Eli's auburn hair had become unfastened, so that it floated carelessly about her; her face was as hot and as red as a berry, her bosom heaved, she could not speak, and laughed because she was so out of breath.

"Yes, that is the way with young people."

Margit looked at Eli with satisfaction as she spoke.

"I suppose you do not know me?"

Eli had no doubt wanted to ask who she was, but could not command the courage to do so, because the other was so much older than she; now she said that she did not remember having seen her before.

"Well, to be sure, that is scarcely to be expected; old folks seldom get out. You may perhaps know my son, Arne Kampen. I am his mother." She stole a sly glance, as she spoke, at Eli, on whom these words wrought a considerable change. "I am inclined to think he worked over at Böen once, did he not?"

Yes, it was Eli's impression, too, that he had done so.

"The weather is fine this evening. We turned our hay to-day, and got it in before I left home; it is really blessed weather."

"There will surely be a good hay-harvest this year," Eli observed.

" Yes, you may well say so. I suppose everything looks splendidly over at Böen."

" They are through harvesting there."

" Oh, of course; plenty of help, stirring people.   Are you going home this evening ? "

No, she did not intend to do so.   They talked together about one thing and another and gradually became so well acquainted that Margit felt at liberty to ask Eli to walk a short distance with her.

" Could you not keep me company a few steps? " said she.   " I so seldom find any one to talk with, and I dare say it will make no difference to you."

Eli excused herself because she had not her jacket on.

" Well, I know, it is really a shame to ask such a thing the first time I meet a person; but then one has to bear with old folks."

Eli said she was quite willing to go, she only wanted to fetch her jacket.

It was a close-fitting jacket; when it was hooked, she looked as if she wore a complete dress; but now she only fastened the two lowest hooks, she was so warm.   Her fine linen had a small turned down collar, and was fastened at the throat with a silver button, in the form of a bird with outspread wings.   Such a one tailor Nils had worn the first time Margit Kampen had danced with him.

"What a handsome button," she remarked, looking at it.

"My mother gave it to me," said Eli.

"Yes, so I thought," and Margit helped the girl adjust it as she spoke.

Now they walked on along the road. The new-mown hay was lying about in heaps. Margit took up a handful, smelled it, and thought it was good. She asked about the live stock at the parsonage, was led thereby to inquire about that at Böen, and then told how much they had at Kampen.

"The gard has prospered finely of late years, and it can be made as much larger as we ourselves wish. It feeds twelve milch cows now, and could feed more; but Arne reads a great many books, and manages according to them, and so he must have his cows fed in a firstrate way."

Eli made no reply to all this, as was quite natural; but Margit asked her how old she was. She was nineteen.

"Have you taken any part in the housework? You look so dainty, I suppose it has not been much."

12

Oh, yes, she had helped in various ways, especially of late.

"Well, it is a good thing to become accustomed to a little of everything; if one should get a large house of one's own, there might be many things to be done. But, to be sure, when one finds good help already in the house, it does not matter so very much."

Eli now thought she ought to turn back, for they had gone far beyond the parsonage lands.

"It will be some time yet before the sun sets; it would be kind if you would chat with me a little longer." And Eli went on.

Then Margit began to talk about Arne. "I do not know if you are very well acquainted with him. He can teach you something about everything. Bless me! how much that boy has read!"

Eli confessed that she was aware he had read a great deal.

"Oh, yes; that is really the least that can be said of him. Why, his conduct to his mother all his days is something far beyond that. If the old saying is true, that one who is good to his mother is sure to be good to his wife, the girl Arne chooses will not have very much to grumble about. What is it you are looking for, child?"

" I only lost a little twig I had in my hand."

They were both silent after this, and walked on without looking at each other.

" He has such strange ways," began the mother, presently; " he was so often frightened when he was a child that he got into the habit of thinking everything over to himself, and such folks never know how to put themselves forward."

Now Eli insisted on turning back, but Margit assured her that it was only a short distance now to Kampen, and see Kampen she must, as she was so near. But Eli thought it was too late that day.

" There is always some one who can go home with you," said Margit.

" No, no," promptly replied Eli, and was about to leave.

" To be sure, Arne is not at home," said Margit; " so it will not be he; but there will be sure to be some one else."

Now Eli had less objection to going; besides, she wanted very much to see Kampen. " If only it does not grow too late," said she.

" Well, if we stand here much longer talking about it, I suppose it may grow too late," and they went on.

" You have read a great deal, I dare say; you who were brought up at the priest's ? "

Yes, Eli had read a good deal.

" That will be useful," Margit suggested,
" when you are married to one who knows less
than you."

Eli thought she would never be married to
such a person.

" Ah, well, it would perhaps not be best
either; but in this parish there is so little
learning."

Eli asked where the smoke rising yonder in
the wood came from.

" It comes from the new houseman's place
belonging to Kampen. A man called Upland
Knut lives there. He was alone in the world,
and so Arne gave him that place to clear. He
knows what it is to be lonely, my poor Arne."

Soon they reached an ascent whence the gard
could be seen. The sun shone full in their
faces; they held up their hands to shade their
eyes and gazed down at Kampen. It lay in the
midst of a plain, the houses red painted and
with white window-frames; the grass in the
surrounding meadows had been mown, the hay
might still be seen in heaps here and there, the
grain-fields lay green and rich among the pale
meadows; over by the cow-house all was stir
and bustle: the cows, sheep, and goats were
just coming home, their bells were tinkling

the dogs were barking, the milk-maids shouting, while above all rose with awful din the roar of the force in the Kamp gorge. The longer Eli looked, the more completely this grand tune filled her ears, and at last it seemed so appalling to her that her heart throbbed wildly; it roared and thundered through her head until she grew bewildered, and at the same time felt so warm and tender that involuntarily she took such short, hesitating steps, that Margit begged her to walk a little faster.

She started. "I never heard anything like that waterfall," said she; " I am almost afraid of it."

" You will soon get used to it," said the mother; "at last you would even miss it if you could not hear it."

"Dear me! do you think so?" cried Eli.

"Well, you will see," said Margit, smiling.

"Come now, let us first look at the cattle," she continued, turning off from the main road. " These trees on each side Nils planted He wanted to have everything nice, Nils did, that is what Arne likes too; look! there you can see the garden my boy has laid out."

" Oh, how pretty!" cried Eli, running over to the garden fence. She had often seen Kampen, but only from a distance, where the garden was not visible.

"We will look at that after a while," said Margit.

Eli hastily glanced through the windows, as she went past the house; there was no one inside.

They stationed themselves on the barn-bridge and watched the cows as they passed lowing into the stable. Margit named them to Eli, told how much milk each one gave, and which of them calved in the summer, which did not. The sheep were counted and let into the fold; they were of a large, foreign breed; Arne had raised them from two lambs he got from the south. "He gives much attention to all such things, although you would not think it of him."

They now went into the barn, and examined the hay that had been housed, and Eli had to smell it — "for such hay is not to be found everywhere." Margit pointed through the barn-hatch over the fields, and told what each one yielded and how much was sown of each kind of seed.

They went out toward the house; but Eli, who had not spoken a word in reply to all that had been said, as they passed by the gar-

den, asked if she might go into it. And when
leave had been given her to go, she begged to
be allowed to pluck a flower or two. There
was a little bench away in one corner; she
went and sat down on it, only to try it, ap-
parently, for she rose at once.

"We must hurry now, if we would not be
too late," said Margit, standing in the door.
And now they went in. Margit asked Eli if
she should offer her some refreshments on this
her first visit; but Eli blushed and hastily declined. Then the girl's eyes wandered all
around the room they had entered; it was
where the family sat in the day-time, and the
windows opened on the road; the room was
not large but it was cozy, and there was a
clock and a stove in it. On the wall hung
Nils's fiddle, dingy and old, but with new
strings. Near it also hung a couple of guns
belonging to Arne, an English angling-rod and
other rare things which the mother took down
and showed to Eli, who looked at them and
handled them. The room was without paint,
for Arne disliked it; nor was there any paint-
ing in the room looking toward the Kamp
gorge, with the fresh green mountains directly
opposite and the blue ones in the background;
this latter room, — which was in the new part

of the building, as was the entire half of the
house it was in, — was larger and prettier than
the first. The two smaller rooms in the wing
were painted, for there the mother was to live
when she was old, and Arne had brought a
wife into the house. They went into the kitch-
en, the store-house, the bake-house, Eli spoke
not a single word; indeed, she viewed everything about her as though from afar off; only
when anything was held out for her inspec-
tion she touched it, but very daintily. Margit, who had kept up an unbroken stream of
chatter the whole way, now led her into the
passage again; they must go and take a look
up-stairs.

There also were well-arranged rooms, cor-
responding with those below; but they were
new and had scarcely yet been occupied, except one, which looked toward the gorge. In
these rooms were kept all sorts of articles
which were not in daily household use. Here
hung a whole lot of robes, together with other
bedclothes; the mother took hold of them, lifted
them up, and now and then insisted on having
Eli do the same. Meanwhile, it actually seemed
as though the young girl were gaining a little
courage, or else her pleasure in these things increased: for to some of them she went back a

second time, asked questions about them, and became more and more interested.

Finally the mother said, "Now at last we will go into Arne's own room;" and then they went into the room overlooking the Kamp gorge. Once more the awful din of the force smote upon their ears, for the window was open. They were up so high that they could see the spray rising between the mountains, but not the force itself, save in one spot farther on, where a fragment had fallen from the cliff, just where the torrent, with all its might, took its final leap into the depths below. Fresh turf covered the upward turned side of this fallen piece of rock, a few fir cones had buried themselves in it, and sent forth a growth of trees with their roots in the crevices. The wind had tugged at and shaken the trees, the force had washed them so completely that there was not a branch four ells from the roots; they were crooked in the knees, their boughs knotted and gnarled, yet they kept their footing, and shot far up between the rocky walls. This was the first thing Eli noticed from the window; the next, the dazzling white snow-capped peaks rising above the green mountains. She turned her eyes away, let them wander over the peaceful, fruitful fields, and finally

about the room where she stood; the roar of
the force had hitherto prevented this.

How calm and cheerful it was within, com-
pared with the scene without. She did not
look at any single article, because one blended
into the other, and most of them were new to
her, for Arne had centred his affections in this
room, and, simple as it was, it was artistic in
almost every particular. It seemed as though
the sound of his songs came floating toward
her, while she stood there, or as though he himself smiled at her from every object. The first
thing her eyes singled out in the room, was a
broad, handsomely carved book-shelf. There
were so many books on it that she did not believe the priest had more. A pretty cabinet
was the next thing she noticed. Here he kept
many rare things, his mother said. Here, too,
he had his money, she added, in a whisper.
They had twice had property left to them, she
told afterwards; they would have one more in-
heritance besides, if things went as they should.
" But money is not the best thing in the world,
after all. Arne may get what is far better."

There were many little trinkets in the room
which were interesting to examine, and Eli
looked at them all, as happy as a child.

Margit patted her on the shoulder, saying, as

she looked brightly into her eyes, "I have
never seen you before to-day, my child, but I
am already very fond of you." Before Eli had
time to feel embarrassed, Margit pulled at her
dress, and said, quite softly, "You see that little red chest; there is something nice in that,
I can tell you."

Eli looked at the chest: it was a small, square
one, which she at once longed to call her own.

"Arne does not want me to know what is in
that chest," whispered the mother, "and he always keeps the key hid." She walked up to
some clothes hanging on the wall, took down a
velvet waistcoat, felt in the watch-pocket, and
there found the key. "Come, now, you shall
see," she whispered.

Eli did not think the mother was doing
quite right, but women are women,—and these
two now crossed softly over to the chest and
knelt in front of it. As the mother raised the
lid, so pleasant a perfume rose toward them that
Eli clapped her hands even before she had seen
anything. Spread over the top was a kerchief
which the mother took away. "Now you shall
see," she whispered, as she took up a fine, black
silk neckerchief, such a one as men do not wear.
"It looks just as if it were for a girl," said the
mother. "Here is another," she added.

Eli could not help taking hold of this; but when the mother insisted upon trying it on her, she declined, and hung her head. The mother carefully folded them up again.

"See!" she then said, taking up some pretty silk ribbons; "everything here looks as if it were meant for a girl."

Eli grew red as fire, but not a sound escaped her; her bosom heaved, her eyes had a shy look, otherwise she stood immovable.

"Here are more things still!" The mother took hold of a beautiful black dress pattern, as she spoke. "This is fine goods, I dare say," said she, as she held it up to the light.

Eli's hands trembled, when the mother asked her to take hold of the cloth, she felt the blood rushing to her head; she would gladly have turned away, but this was not easy to do.

"He has bought something every time he has been to town," said the mother.

Eli could scarcely control herself any longer; her eyes roamed about the chest from one article to another, and back again to the dress goods; she, in fact, saw nothing else. But the mother persisted, and the last thing she took up was wrapped in paper; they slowly unwrapped it; this became attractive again. Eli grew eager; it proved to be a pair of small

shoes. They had never seen anything like
these, either one of them; the mother won-
dered how they could be made. Eli said nothing, but when she went to touch the shoes,
all her fingers made marks on them; she felt so
ashamed that she came very near bursting into
tears. She longed most of all to take her
leave, but she dared not speak, nor dare she
do anything to make the mother look up.

Margit was wholly occupied with her own
thoughts. "Does it not look just as if he had
bought them one by one for some one he had
not the courage to give them to?" said she, as
she put each article back in the place where
she had found it; she must have had practice
in so doing. "Now let us see what there is in
this little box," she added, softly opening it, as
though now they were going to find something
really choice.

There lay a buckle, broad enough for a belt;
that was the first thing she showed Eli; the
next was two gold rings, tied together, and
then the girl caught sight of a velvet hymn-book
with silver clasps; further she could not look,
for on the silver of the book was engraved, in
small letters, "Eli, Baardsdatter Böen."[1]

Margit called her attention to something, got

[1] The Norse word *datter* means daughter.

no reply, but saw that tear after tear was trickling down on the silk kerchief, and spreading over it. Then the mother laid down the brooch she held in her hand, closed the little box, turned round and clasped Eli in her arms. The daughter wept on her shoulder, and the mother wept over her, but neither of them spoke a word.

A little while later, Eli was walking alone in the garden ; the mother had gone into the kitchen to prepare something good for supper, for now Arne would soon be home. By and by, Margit came out into the garden to look for her young friend, and found her sitting writing in the sand. As the mother joined her, Eli quickly smoothed the sand over what she had written, — looked up and smiled; she had been weeping.

"There is nothing to cry about, my child," said Margit, and gave her a pat.

They saw a black object moving between the bushes on the road. Eli stole into the house, the mother followed her. Here a bounteous repast was awaiting them : cream pudding, smoked meat, and cakes; but Eli had no eyes for these things ; she crossed the floor to the corner where the clock stood, sat down on a chair close to the wall, and trembled if she only heard a cat stir. The mother stood by the table. Firm steps were heard on the flagstones, a short, light step in the passage, the door was gently opened, and Arne came in.

The first object his eyes lighted on was Eli in the clock corner; he let go of the door and stood still. This made Eli yet more embarrassed; she got up, regretted at once having done so, and turned towards the wall.

"Are *you* here?" said Arne, softly, blushing crimson.

Eli shaded her eyes with one hand, as one does when the sun shines too full in the face.

"How —?" He could get no farther, but he advanced a step or two.

She put her hand down again, turned toward him, then, bowing her head, she burst into tears.

"God bless you, Eli!" said he, and drew his arm around her; she nestled close up to him. He whispered something in her ear; she made no reply, but clasped her hands about his neck.

They stood thus for a long time, and not a sound was heard save the roar of the force, sending forth its eternal song. By and by some one was heard weeping near the table Arne looked up: it was the mother.

"Now I am sure you will not leave me, Arne," said she, approaching him. She wept freely, but it did her good, she said.

When Arne and Eli walked home together in the bright summer evening, they did not talk much about their new-born happiness. They let Nature herself take the lead in the conversation, — so quiet, bright, and grand, she seemed, as she accompanied them. But it was on his way back to Kampen from this their first summer-night's walk, with his face turned toward the rising sun, that he laid the foundations of a poem, which he was then in no frame of mind to construct, but which, later, when it was finished, became for a while his daily song. It ran thus: —

"I hoped to become something great one day;
I thought it would be when I got away.
Each thought that my bosom entered
On far-off journeys was centred.
A maiden then into my eyes did look;
My rovings soon lost their pleasure.
The loftiest aim my heart can brook
Is her to proclaim my treasure.

"I hoped to become something great one day;
I thought it would be when I got away.
To meet with the great in learning
Intensely my heart was yearning.
She taught me, she did, for she spoke a word:
'The best gift of God's bestowing

Is not to be called a distinguished lord,
But ever a *man* to be growing.

" I hoped to become something great one day ;
I thought it would be when I got away.
My home seemed so cold, neglected,
I felt like a stranger suspected.
When her I discovered, then love I did see
    In every glance that found me ;
Wherever I turned friends waited for me,
    And life became new around me."

There came afterwards many a summer evening walk, followed by many a song. One of these must be recorded : —

" The cause of this all is beyond my knowing ;
No storm there has been and no floods have been flowing.
A sparkling and glittering brook, it would seem,
Has poured itself into the broader stream
Which constantly growing seeks the ocean.

" There is something we can from our lives not sever ;
In need it is near and forsakes us never, —
A power that draws, a loving breast,
Which sadness, shyness, and all unrest
Can gather in peace in a bridal present.

" Could I but by spirits through life be attended,
As pure as the thought which has now me befriended !
The ordering spirit of God it was.
He ruleth the world with sacred laws.
Toward goodness eternal I am progressing."

But perhaps none of them better expressed his fervent gratitude than the following : —

" The power that gave me my little song
    Has caused that as rain has been my sadness,
    And that as sunshine has been my gladness,
The spring-time wants of my soul along.
        Whate'er betided
        It did no harm;
        My song all guided
        To love so warm.

" The power that gave me my little song
    Has given me friendship for all that 's yearning
    For freedom's blessings my blood is burning;
The foe I am of every wrong.
        I sought my station,
        Spite every storm,
        And found salvation
        In love so warm.

" The power that gave me my little song
    Must make me able to sing the others,
    And now and then to make glad my brothers
Whom I may meet in the worldly throng,—
        For there was never
        A sweeter charm
        Than singing ever
        In love so warm."

CHAPTER XVI.

IT was late in the autumn; the harvesters were at work housing the grain. The day was clear, it had rained during the night; and in the morning, therefore, the air was as mild as in summer-time. It was a Saturday, and yet many boats were making their way across Black Water toward the church; the men, in their shirt sleeves, were rowing; the women sat in the stern, with light-colored kerchiefs on their heads. A still greater number of boats were steering over to Böen, in order to move away from there later in grand procession, for on this day Baard Böen gave a wedding for his daughter Eli and Arne Nils' son Kampen.

All the doors were open; people were going in and out; children, with pieces of cake in their hands, stood about the yard, afraid of their new clothes, and looking shyly at one another; an old woman sat upon the store-house steps alone, — it was Margit Kampen. She wore a large silver ring, with several small rings fastened to the upper silver plate; now

and then she looked at it ; Nils had given it to
her the day of their wedding and she had never
worn it since.

The man who presided at the feast, and the
two young groomsmen, the priest's son and
Eli's brother, went about in the two or three
rooms, offering refreshments to the wedding
guests as they arrived to be present on this
great occasion. Up-stairs in Eli's room were
the bride, the priest's wife, and Mathilde, —
the last-named had come from town for the
sole purpose of decking the bride; this the
girls had promised each other from their childhood.   Arne — wearing a broadcloth suit, with
close-fitting roundabout and with a collar that
Eli had made — stood in one of the down-stairs
rooms by the window on which Eli had written
" Arne."

Outside in the passage two persons met as
they came each from some duty of the day.
One of them was on his way from the landing-
place, where he had been helping to put the
church boats in order ; he wore a black broadcloth roundabout, with blue wadmal trousers,
whose dye rubbed off, so that his hands were
blue ; his white collar looked well with his fair
face and long light hair ; his high forehead was
calm ; about the mouth played a smile.   It was

Baard. She whom he met in the passage was
just coming from the kitchen. She was dressed
for church, was tall and slender, and walked
with a firm though hurried step through the
door. When she met Baard she paused, and
her mouth drew up to one side. It was Birgit,
his wife. Each had something to say, but it
only found expression through both standing
still. Baard was the most embarrassed of the
two; he smiled more and more, but it was his
embarrassment that came to his aid, forcing
him to start up-stairs without further delay.
"Perhaps you will come too," he said, as he
passed, and Birgit followed him. Up-stairs in
the garret they were entirely alone; yet Baard
locked the door after them, and he was a long
time about it. When finally he turned, Birgit
stood by the window gazing out; it was in
order to avoid looking into the room. Baard
brought forth a small flask from his breast
pocket and a little silver cup. He wanted to
pour out some wine for his wife, but she would
not have any, although he assured her that it
was wine that had been sent from the parsonage. Then he drank himself, but paused several times to offer the cup to her. He corked
the flask, put both it and the cup away in his
breast-pocket again, and sat down on a chest.

It very evidently pained him that his wife
would not drink with him.

He breathed heavily several times. Birgit
stood leaning with one hand against the window frame. Baard had something to say, but
now it seemed even harder to speak than before.

"Birgit!" said he, "I dare say you are thinking of the same to-day that I am."

Then he heard her move from one side of the
window to the other, and again she leaned her
head on her arm.

"Oh, yes; you know who I mean. He it
was who parted us two. I thought it would
not go beyond the wedding, but it has lasted
much longer."

He heard her sigh, he saw her again change
her place; but he did not see her face. He
himself was struggling so hard that he had to
wipe his face with his jacket sleeve. After a
long conflict he began again : " To-day a son
of his, well-educated and handsome, becomes
one of us, and to him we have given our only
daughter. Now, how would it be, Birgit, if we
two were to have our wedding to-day ? "

His voice trembled, and he cleared his throat.
Birgit, who had raised her head, now leaned it
on her arm again, but said nothing. Baard

waited for some time; he heard her breathe, but he got no answer, — and he had nothing further to say himself either. He looked up and grew very pale; for she did not even turn her head. Then he rose.

At the same moment there was a gentle knock at the door, and a soft voice asked, "Are you coming, mother?" It was Eli. There was something in the tone that made Baard involuntarily pause and glance at Birgit. Birgit also raised her head; she looked towards the door, and her eyes fell on Baard's pale face. "Are you coming, mother?" was once more asked from without.

"Yes, I am coming now!" said Birgit, in a broken voice, as she firmly crossed the floor to where Baard stood, gave him her hand, and burst into the most passionate weeping. The two hands met, they were both toil-worn now, but they clasped as firmly as though they had been seeking each other for twenty years. They still clung together as they went toward the door, and when a while later the bridal procession was passing down to the landing-place, and Arne gave his hand to Eli to take the lead, Baard, seeing it, took his wife by the hand, contrary to all custom, and followed them, smiling contentedly.

Behind them, Margit Kampen walked alone, as was her wont.

Baard was in high spirits that day; he sat talking with the rowers. One of these who kept looking up at the mountains remarked, that it was strange that even such a steep rock could be clad.

" It must, whether it would or no," said Baard, and his eyes wandered all along the procession until they rested on the bridal pair and his wife. " Who could have foretold this twenty years ago ? " said he.